Happy 75th birthday. Dad
love Eulian, Phi

# Sabbath Morn

Rogate-on-Sands is a seaside town whose population consists mainly of the retired and whose economy is heavily reliant on the annual influx of summer visitors. Its small police force copes efficiently with the petty crime which comes its way, rarely having to deal with anything more serious than shoplifting or drunk and disorderlies on a Saturday night.

Sunday, July 7th, drastically alters that complacency.

The day dawns hazily, holding the promise of sunshine and soaring temperatures. The day shift starts with the unusual problem of identifying a stray donkey who has consumed a large percentage of the floral display in the corporation gardens. It is to prove the only light moment of the day, because within an hour of the start of the new shift a police constable has been murdered and a siege has developed. A situation which threatens to get rapidly out of hand.

Then, with the small force already at full stretch, there is a rash of arson attacks in the town, and a mysterious stranger keeps appearing in very unlikely places.

John Wainwright's masterly touch brings to life the intricacies of policing, the network of a community and the effects of violence on ordinary people. He has mixed the ordinary with the abnormal and the result is a wholly credible, gripping crime novel.

# SABBATH MORN

## JOHN WAINWRIGHT

LITTLE, BROWN AND COMPANY

A *Little, Brown* Book

First published in Great Britain in 1993
by Little, Brown and Company

A CIP catalogue record for this book is available
from the British Library.

ISBN 0 316 90479 1

Photoset in North Wales by
Derek Doyle & Associates, Mold, Clwyd.
Printed and bound in Great Britain by
Mackays of Chatham PLC, Chatham, Kent

Little, Brown and Company (UK) Limited
165 Great Dover Street
London SE1 4YA

*This one is for Mike and Jean*

# SUNDAY, July 7th

## *0545 Hours*

Joe Blythe did what he always did on a morning like this. When he was within sight of the police station, he swung right, crossed the road, crossed Rock Walk, crossed the promenade, then stood with one foot resting on the bottom bar of the railings and gazed out to sea.

It was a routine. Like emptying his bladder, like filling and switching on the kettle before he returned to the bathroom for a shave, like opening the front door and eyeing the clouds as he brought in the morning milk. It was part of the beginning of a good day, and Joe Blythe liked good days.

It was, he decided, going to be hot. Bloody hot. The weathermen had promised it. Somewhere, out in the Atlantic, a great bank of cloud was edging its way west, but whether the present high would allow it passage was anybody's guess. And, if it did, it was going to be another forty-eight hours before any rain crossed the Irish Sea.

Meanwhile it was going to be another scorcher. And from eleven o'clock the pubs would be serving liquid refreshment, and the younger holiday-makers would

1

happily grow more drunk by the minute. And somebody would say something, or maybe do something, calculated to upset an already wobbly apple-cart and, for another day, the long-suffering coppers would be piggy-in-the-middle.

So ride the day at its own speed, squire. Fill your lungs with good sea air. Don't forget that a few thousand people are paying good money to be here in Rogate-on-Sands. This is the place they've dreamed about for the last fifty weeks or so. This is what they've been saving money for. And you, squire, are *paid* to be here. Not for a week. Not for a fortnight. This is where you work, and this is where you live. You are a very lucky man and, if you don't think you *are* a lucky man, remember Brum and the industrial muck they'll be filling their lungs with there.

Thus the thoughts of Police Sergeant 1010 Joseph Blythe.

Despite what would come later, the morning air had a slight post-dawn chill. It wasn't actually cold, but there was the hint of a mist – a 'heat haze' was what the locals called it – and there was enough residual night moisture in the air to bring on a touch of gooseflesh.

The tide was out, and on the turn. Blythe could see the scalloped edge of the waves as they crept up the sand, but he couldn't see the horizon. The mist seemed to thicken slightly over the sea, until it took on the consistency of candy-floss.

It was, Blythe decided, a little like a Turner painting.

A great, awkward pup, whose ancestors had included red setters, lolloped across the sand. It seemed not to have full control of its legs. They were like doors with broken hinges caught in a gale, flapping and waving as they pleased. The dog was chasing a thrown ball and, as it skidded to a sand-spraying halt, it lost what little balance it had and rolled onto its side.

2

Blythe switched his attention from the dog to the man throwing the ball. He looked and he took careful notice, as opposed to merely seeing. It was a conscious, positive act, and it brought the man into sharp focus for future reference. Late twenties or early thirties. Moderate build. Moderate height. Sandy-coloured hair bordering upon ginger. Short, high back-and-sides, with the top straightened off to near crew-cut. Clean-shaven. No specs. Royal blue track-suit, with a dark red stripe down the sides of the trousers and the sleeves. No logo. White sneakers. Not a casual jogger. More of a keep-fit fanatic. Shoulders back. Head up. Elbows hard into the sides. Legs pumping and knees lifting high. The man ran in short, fast bursts of speed. When he wasn't moving forward and when he wasn't throwing the ball for the dog to retrieve, he was doing a fast, running-on-the-spot routine.

Blythe's lips moved into a slow, sardonic smile.

'Typical,' he murmured gently. 'Typical army muscle-wallah.'

And maybe that's what the man was. It was possible. What he wasn't was somebody Blythe had seen before. He wasn't one of the regular early morning crowd. Not from the railway, or one of the bus depot lads. Not a Post Office worker on his way in, or a milk delivery chap, or one of the kitchen staff employed by the hotels.

Like every other copper who'd worked a shift system for a fair length of time, Blythe knew all the 'official' early-risers, the men and women he might meet at this hour in the morning. He knew where they were going; in many cases, he knew where they lived.

But not this one.

He wasn't from one of the hotels. The stupidly behaved dog ruled that out. Most of the hotels didn't take dogs, and those that did reserved the right to refuse if the dog was too big or too bouncy. And this one *was*. Much too big. Much too bouncy.

Nor was he from one of the guest houses – what used to be called 'boarding houses' – because seaside landladies (even Rogate-on-Sands landladies) didn't go in for 5.30 a.m. ball games. Of course, the up-bright-and-early holi ¹y-maker sometimes liked a pre-breakfast stroll. A quick sniff of the sea air. A call for an early morning coffee. To pick up a favourite newspaper. That sort of thing. But not before half-past seven. Those landladies and their husbands served breakfast at nine (and not before) and their front doors weren't unlocked for exit or entrance before half-past seven.

Blythe stared at the man and his idiot dog, and muttered, 'You're a puzzler, old son. Whoever you are, you're a puzzler.'

Police Constable 199 Howes could never quite make himself *look* like a copper. It had a lot to do with his general physiognomy. He wore the uniform. He strolled the pavements at the regulation saunter. Occasionally he reported somebody for summons. These things didn't mean a thing. He neither looked the part nor acted the part.

In many respects Howes was a walking, talking optical illusion. He didn't look tall enough to be a policeman. As sure as hell, he didn't look broad enough or strong enough. He allowed his hair to grow slightly longer than regulations encouraged and he sported a full set of whiskers. Because of some imbalance in his bodily make-up the hair had been Persil-white since his teenage years. Put a police helmet atop that lot and the immediate impression was of a fugitive from an amateur production of a Snow White pantomime.

Howes arrived at Rogate-on-Sands Police Station, paused at the foot of the shallow steps leading up to the entrance, looked up at the front of the particularly unlovely pile and indulged in one of his more curious, but quite harmless, foibles. He talked to an inanimate object.

He breathed, 'You ugly bastard.'

Then he climbed the steps and entered the world of law enforcement.

Section Police Sergeant Stanningly looked up from the public counter and grumbled, 'You lot are never too eager, are you?'

'Eh?' Howes blinked.

'You're supposed to parade fifteen minutes before going onto the streets. So far you're the only one to turn up.'

'They'll be here, Sergeant. They'll be here in time to parade.'

'It's *already* time to parade.'

Stanningly was a griper. Renowned as such. Give him some slight cause for complaint, and he made a five-course meal out of it. He'd been on duty since ten o'clock the previous evening. It had been one of those a-lot-of-fiddling-about-for-nothing sort of nights – a stupid 'domestic disturbance' in which a man's common law wife had pushed her luck to the absolute limit, a nine-nine-niner set off because a fancy burglar alarm had been tripped by a mouse or a rat or something, and couldn't be switched off without the palaver of raising the key-holder, and then the bloody donkey . . . it had been one of those nights Stanningly could have done without.

He growled, 'It's there in black and white. Force Orders. Fifteen minutes before going on duty. Parade.'

'They'll be here, Sergeant.'

'They're *not* here. Nobody's here. That's what I'm on about.'

'I'll take over,' volunteered Howe.

5

'What?'

'I'll hold the fort until—'

'The hell you will!'

'Eh?'

'If you think I'm going to leave Rogate in the hands of a prize prat like you—'

'Away home, Edgar. Climb between cool sheets.' Blythe arrived and spoke as he lifted the counter flap and joined his fellow sergeant. He turned to Howes. 'Into the Parade Room, Wilf. Take the Telephone Book. Check the messages, and let me know what's important when I join you.'

'Yes, Sergeant.'

Stanningly said, 'You're late.'

'Hardly,' smiled Blythe.

'I don't suppose it's important.' Stanningly spoke as if forgiving a great sin. He pulled a large, blue-tinted form nearer along the top of the counter. He tapped the form in the appropriate places as he continued. 'Barstow. Tim Barstow. Drunk and Disorderly. No real trouble. We picked him up at about midnight.'

'As always. Every week.'

'Saturday night,' agreed Stanningly. 'He's banged up. His wife's been told. She'd like him bailed in time for church. I promised we'd do our best.'

'I'll see to it. Anything else?'

'A stray donkey.'

'*What?*'

'Playing havoc with the flower beds in Rock Walk. It took some bloody catching. It's in the dog pound ... when we find the owner.'

'What about foddering it?'

'It doesn't need fodder,' said Stanningly sourly. 'It's eaten enough flowers to keep it satisfied for a week.'

'Anything else I should know?'

'Crosby went to bed early. Before half-past ten. That

6

could mean he'll be on the prowl early.'

'Uh-huh.' Blythe nodded, then said, 'A copper-headed chap. Thirty-ish. Blue track-suit. Has a damn great pup with him. He's doing physical jerks on the sands.'

'Now?' Stanningly raised an eyebrow. 'At this time?'

'As I came in.'

'It doesn't ring bells.' Stanningly shook his head.

Blythe sighed and said, 'I'll maybe check him out.' He glanced through the window and added, 'It's going to be another grid-iron session today. Once it starts, we'll all sweat buckets.'

## 0600 Hours

Like every other fuzz-palace in the United Kingdom, Rogate-on-Sands Police Station was bulging with buckshee coppers at this o'clock. The Night Shift was signing off and the Early Shift was signing on. This didn't happen at two o'clock. It didn't happen at ten o'clock. The ten-six Day Shift stitched together the Early and the Afternoon Shifts. The six-two Late Shift did the same for the Afternoon and the Night periods.

It was slightly crazy. In effect, it meant that any moderately enterprising car thief or house-breaker could be sure that he had the freedom of the streets for about thirty minutes, if only he shook the dust of sleep from his eyes early enough.

Crazy or not, it was the police way. The day started and ended at 6 a.m. Those first six hours of every day were, officially, part of the previous day's timescale. A fresh start. A clean slate. And at six o'clock – fifteen minutes before and fifteen minutes after – every working shift copper was safely tucked away in his own little nick, bleary-eyed from having been awake all night

7

or still drowsy from having just crawled from his bed.

It was a great time for lawlessness.

In the Parade Room Blythe was saying, 'The usual. A quick nip round the unoccupied property first thing. The lock-ups. Make sure nobody's been trying for Early Morning Gallops.'

Six men were in the Parade Room listening to Blythe's spiel. Four beat constables. The old man of the section, Constable Vine, anxious to take over cell duty while there was an occupant of the lock-up; anxious because the first thing he had to do was organise the prisoner's breakfast . . . which included organising his own breakfast. The sixth man was Police Constable 989 Robert Grafton, and his job was to perform switchboard duty and keep the clerical work ticking over, pending the arrival of the civilian clerk at nine.

The other four men were responsible for A, B, C and D Beats respectively.

' . . . and make sure you've all noted the registration numbers of circulated stolen vehicles. Nicked Saturday night. They're usually abandoned by Sunday morning.' Blythe paused, then said, 'Howes, you're on A Beat.'

'Yes, Sergeant.'

'There's a character on the beach. Gingerish hair. Blue track-suit. He has a bloody great dog with him. A setter, or something. If he's still around, chat him up a bit. Find what you can.'

'Y'mean name? Address?'

'At least that.'

'What if he won't give them?'

'Oh, for Christ's sake!' Blythe lifted his gaze to heaven. 'Don't just *ask* . . . not like that. Kid him along a bit. You're a copper. Touch your helmet to him. Natter on about the weather. That you hope he enjoys his holiday . . . '

'What if he isn't . . . '

8

'If he isn't, he'll *say* he isn't. Tell him what a handsome sod he is . . . '

'Sergeant, I don't think I'll . . . '

'Anything. Use your imagination. Just get him talking. Then pump him as dry as you can.'

Blythe wished he'd strolled down to the sands to talk with the track-suited stranger. It would, of course, have meant him being late at the nick, and Stanningly would have had something else to moan about. But there was something fishy about the keep-fit lad. Something not quite plumb. Just *something*. But it was too late now, and maybe Howes wasn't quite as dim as he made himself out to be.

He said, 'The rest of you. B, C and D Beats. Keep on your toes. Be where you *should* be. A birdie tells me the super's likely to be sniffing around . . . and before the streets have been aired.'

Charlie Daniels worried away at the same old problem, like a terrier worrying away at a bone too big for its jaws. Since ten o'clock last night he'd worried at it all around B Beat. And now it was past six o'clock, he'd left his tunic in the Locker Room, exchanged it for a lightweight sports jacket – and he was still worrying at it as he made his way home and to bed.

To bed? Who the hell was he kidding? Maybe to bed, but, for sure, no chance of sleep. If he, Charlie Daniels, knew anything, he'd be tossing around between the sheets going over every pro and con he'd already been over a hundred times already.

It was a nice proposition. It was a very tempting proposition, and maybe – just *maybe* – they could make a real go of it. Chris, Beth and himself. Just the three of them. With what they could already scrape together, plus a second mortgage on the house, plus a bigger dollop of luck than anybody had the right to expect.

They could maybe pull it. They would maybe have enough cash to see them off the launch pad. They just might. But all those 'mights'. And all those 'maybes'.

Chris was so damned sure.

'It's a snip, Charlie,' he'd enthused. 'A garage. All the gear. A going concern. Welding. Panel-beating. Forecourt. Bags of work-space. House attached. A nice, big house. You and Beth could live there. Separate rooms . . . that sort of thing. I'd just be a lodger – a paying guest – until we'd had the place altered.'

'I could do the pumps.' Beth had been just as enthusiastic. 'And Chris *is* a mechanic. Qualified, not one of those been-to-the-manufacturing-plant mechanics. Not a big-hammer expert.'

And all that was no less than the truth. Chris *was* a whiz-kid when it came to motor-car engines. When it came to anything to do with motor-cars. He'd proved it at the Poly. He'd proved it, again and again, at Rogate's main garage. He wasn't yet thirty, but already he was their top man. Their consultant. The mechanic the management always ran to with their problems.

Fine, but he was also *Chris*.

Chris was Charlie Daniels' younger brother and, as far back as he could remember, Chris had looked after Number One. Bugger the others . . . let them go under. Just as long as *he* stayed afloat. Always. More than that, he'd never even had the simple bottle to keep grafting when things turned a little rough. He'd always wanted out, always insisted upon being the first one in the lifeboat.

It was why, years ago, Beth had given Chris the bum's rush and moved over to the elder brother. Why she'd become Mrs *Charlie* Daniels. Because, as a husband, Chris would have been the world's greatest non-starter.

And now this.

For the three of them to take over a garage.

10

A snip for a quick sale. Ticking over, and primed for a great future. The chance of complete independence, and the promise of money – *real* money – in a few years' time.

That, or being a copper for the next twenty years. Maybe a sergeant. A faint possibility of making the rank of inspector. A rock-solid, no-risk future. A good pension, and retirement at an age when he could take on a nice, easy-going, part-time job to pay for the few little luxuries of life.

It wasn't an easy decision.

Instead of turning right into Bank Street and from there along Abingdon Road, to where his bed awaited, Daniels turned left into West Lane, then right along Churchill Avenue until he reached the garage.

The present owner was just opening up.

He was a little guy – a shade more than five feet six inches – and he wore a chocolate-coloured suit, complete with waistcoat. He wore a chocolate-coloured trilby and brown shoes, polished to a high shine. He wore a shirt without a collar and no tie. His general expression was one of perpetual impatience. Charlie Daniels figured him to be a few degrees too sullen to make a success of any business.

The owner scowled a little, then said, 'You as well?'

'I'm sorry. I don't . . . '

'The other one's been here already.'

'The other one?'

'Who is he? Your brother?'

'Oh. Chris.'

'He was here when I arrived. Snooping around. Parking that damn great Merc by the pumps. You want to make your mind up.'

'Yeah.' Charlie Daniels nodded.

'I've had other offers, y'know.'

'Yeah.'

11

'I can't keep it open for ever.'

'No. Of course not. That's – y'know – understood.'

'Nice day.' Constable Howes tried to kick-start some sort of conversation. As an afterthought he added, 'It's going to be hot again.'

'It's going to be hot again,' agreed the man in the blue track-suit.

The dog bounded down the slope and back to the beach, then twisted, turned and raced back up the slope to the prom and its master.

'Maybe a bit too hot,' tried Howes. 'I mean – y'know – it can be too hot.'

'Can it?'

'Yes. Well, no . . . not if you like heat. I mean, if you like heat, it can never be too hot. Can it?'

'I don't mind.' The man threw the ball onto the sands and the dog raced down the slope again. He asked, 'Do you?'

'What?'

'Mind?'

'Mind what?'

'The heat.'

'Yes. Well . . . no. Not the heat.'

'Good.'

'Eh? Oh – er – yes.' Howes moved his lips together in an attempt to remove the dryness and moisten them. It made his beard waggle. This made him look more ridiculous than ever. He blurted out, 'Are you – I mean, do you . . . are you on holiday?'

'No. Why?'

'I just – y'know – just wondered.'

'Really?'

'A lot of people are.'

The dog returned, dropped the ball and pranced around, waiting for somebody to throw the ball back

12

onto the sands.

Howes mumbled, 'Do you – I mean, would you . . . do you mind telling me who you are?'

'Who *I* am?' The man stopped and pocketed the ball.

'Who – y'know . . . your name and address.'

'Why?'

'It's just that, y'know . . . ' Howes took a deep breath, then said, 'It's my sergeant. He – he saw you. On the beach, not long ago. He – y'know . . . he doesn't *know* you.'

'Should he?'

'He knows most people.'

'I saw him, by the rails.'

'So . . . ' Howes sounded a little desperate. 'Do you mind? Telling me who you are, I mean?'

'I mind,' said the man solemnly. 'I mind, if only because your sergeant doesn't seem to like doing his own dirty work. I also mind because, at the moment, I have no means of identification. I could give you a false name, and a false address, and there isn't a thing you could do about it. You wouldn't even know.'

'No, sir. But if you'd . . . '

'What I will do,' offered the man with a smile. 'At ten o'clock I'll call in at the police station, complete with evidence of identity. And if your sergeant is still curious, I'll identify myself to him.'

## *0615 Hours*

D Beat was the residential beat. It could have been an average police beat in any moderately prosperous part of any city or town. It was a nice mix of 'Bungalow Land' and 'Flat Land'. It had a history. Once upon a time, when Great King Cotton ruled towns like Oldham and Blackburn, Burnley and Bolton, the fat cats who'd

13

owned the mills had built themselves mini-mansions in the north-west coastal resorts. Rambling places in reasonable grounds, but with a multiplicity of rooms, large and high-ceilinged, in which to house large families, and a series of tiny attics and cellars in which to house the servants. Personal statements of wealth, constructed in best, Accrington brick.

Then King Cotton moved his throne to India, and his Lancastrian courtiers felt the draught. The ridiculous mansions of Southport and Lytham-St-Annes, of Morecambe and Cleveleys, of Rogate-on-Sands and Bispham came up for grabs. Some had been turned into small hotels and guest houses. Some were private nursing homes and retirement homes. Some had been turned into flats. Some had been razed to the ground, and purpose-built flats had been built on the plots. And where the small but adequate grounds had once been, there had been built luxury and near-luxury bungalows.

The result was D Beat, plus a few hundred other D Beats up and down the coast, and about half a mile inland from various proms.

'It puzzles me,' observed Blythe.

'What?'

'Where they go when they want a quick pint.'

'They rarely do.' PC Walker grinned. 'This is where Shaw's 'Middle-class Morality' lives. You're up to the elbows in it here. A few notches up and they'd be away to the wine bars and night clubs. A few notches down and they'd sit comfortably in the snugs of decent pubs. But not here. Not at this level. Here, it's home boozing, and occasionally out for an evening meal with wine and drinks later.'

'No pubs,' sighed Blythe.

'Just the one.'

'Ah, yes. The Jester's Bells.' Blythe nodded. 'I

14

suppose that's as near as you'll get to a local round here. A fancy name for a fancy drinking-hole.'

Walker said, 'It's made to measure. Made to order. Some genius worked out exactly what they wanted – exactly what they'd *allow* themselves – then provided it. Not quite a cafeteria. Not quite a carvery. Slightly more up-market than the average pub lunch. A mixture of all three . . . and at pensioners' rate. And in a very select room where you can eat your lunch and drink your beer in the company of your own kind. It's very popular, Sergeant. And rightly so.'

'If you say so.'

'It helps keep them sane.'

Walker wasn't far from retirement, and for the last twelve years he'd worked only D Beat. Blythe accepted the assessment of a man not given to wild theories.

Walker continued, 'Ex-colonials. Retired officers of middle rank. Fixed incomes, and even more fixed opinions. That's what you have here, Sergeant. Given a choice they'd live in Brighton, Bournemouth or Hastings. Somewhere on the south coast, within easy distance of London. That's where they'd like to live . . . it's where they'd like to afford to live. But they haven't saved, and they lack the expertise to do anything capable of bringing in an even reasonable salary.'

'They're well-educated dumb-bells. Is that what you're saying?'

'Not quite. But they just can't change their ways. All their life they've had servants – maybe batmen – to carry the sticks and fetch the water. Now they haven't, and they're lost. They're pretty helpless. Toast and marmalade . . . anything more involved than that and they're off to The Jester's Bells. And if they can't afford *that*, they starve. But in a quiet, genteel way. The one thing they refuse to do is make a nuisance of themselves.'

15

'That can't be right.' Blythe shook his head. 'Not today.'

'It's right . . . near enough.' Walker's voice was heavy with sad assurance.

'Nobody starves these days. Hell's teeth, the so-called Welfare State makes sure—'

'They won't accept charity.'

'Who the hell's talking about "charity". I'm not . . .'

'That's what they call it. And nobody can argue them out of that belief. As you say, they needn't starve but they *will* starve. From choice, rather than answer questions asked by some petty local bureaucrat.'

Blythe's brow furrowed in puzzlement. He accepted the opinion without much argument, but he couldn't understand what he, personally, figured as a cock-eyed state of affairs.

Blythe liked Johnny Walker. Of all the coppers at Rogate, Walker was the most dependable. He pulled his weight, sometimes more than his weight. He didn't need 'supervising' all the time. Leave him alone, let him get on with his job of looking after D Beat in his own quiet way, and nobody was ever likely to have much to complain about.

And because Walker was both civilised and gentle company, Blythe had left the police station shortly after six, and strolled to D Beat for what, in police jargon, was known as a 'company visit'. The time and place of their meeting would be recorded in Walker's notebook. When Blythe left him, their parting place and time would, again, be recorded. It was a sergeant/copper relationship which, no doubt, had started with Peel and would continue while law-enforcement was necessary.

The slight difference in rank meant nothing; it was more than compensated for by the difference in age. Blythe *liked* Walker and believed that the feeling was reciprocated.

16

They talked, then, as equals. They talked softly, if only because of the hour, the temperature and the fact that bedroom windows had been left open in an attempt to beat the humidity of the night. Their talk was interrupted, usually once, sometimes twice, in each street they patrolled. Walker swung from the pavement, opened a garden gate, walked up the path and round the building. The building was usually a bungalow. He tried each door and glanced at each window. He was doing his job. He was 'checking the property' of citizens who were away from home.

They turned into Audsley Avenue. Their pace didn't alter. They continued exchanging opinions and small talk. They reached Number Twenty-Six and, again, Walker opened the gate and strolled down the drive. Blythe waited on the footpath.

It was a bungalow. High-roofed and tall-chimneyed. It had twin bay windows and the panes were leaded. It had a bigger than usual garden, and the garden was walled to the height of six foot along the sides and at the rear. The garden was mainly lawn with, here and there, a well-established tree. There were a couple of apple trees, an almond tree, a copper beech, a willow and two mountain ashes ... and Walker was taking an uncommonly long time to check a simple, unoccupied property.

Crosby wished to hell he hadn't reached last evening's decision. He also wished to hell he'd kept his mouth shut and not voiced that decision to his wife.

In an unusually expansive and self-assured mood, he'd said, 'I think I'll check the early morning men tomorrow.'

His wife had smiled her approval, and replied, 'What a good idea, Andrew. It's a long time since you made your presence felt before ten o'clock.'

17

Nor had her words been in any way sarcastic. She was the daughter of a small-force chief constable. She was also the sister of a Met superintendent. She had the purest of police blood flowing through her veins, and was ridiculously proud of the fact. Indeed, and in many ways, she was a better copper than he was.

Andrew Lewis Crosby. He was a uniformed Police Superintendent, and the man in charge of Rogate-on-Sands Police Division. On his more honest days – on one of the few days when he wasn't making himself look mildly stupid via self-deception – Crosby might have admitted that he'd never been cut out to be a policeman. That having joined and having discovered exactly what the job entailed, wisdom should have sent him scooting into his then DHQ, clutching a hastily made-out resignation form. He might have been a happier man. A more fulfilled man. A less vaguely miserable man.

Instead, and as always, he'd dithered and delayed matters. Then he'd married and been promoted Sergeant, in that order. Maybe because of the woman he'd married, maybe because he'd kept his nose uncommonly clean, if only because he'd done so little to dirty it, he'd made Inspector, then Chief Inspector and, finally, Superintendent.

But nobody knew better than Crosby himself that, although he held the rank, and although he was the divisional officer, he was a few light years short of being a real copper.

Nevertheless, periodically (as last night) he made believe he was.

And now, in the bright, pristine light of an immediate post-dawn, he wished to hell he'd kept his mouth shut.

They'd gone to bed a little earlier than usual, but at this hour in the morning that didn't mean much. If you've grown used to climbing out of bed at nine, it doesn't matter a damn what time you retire; six o'clock

18

remains three hours too soon.

He stood under the shower, raised his face to the spray and kept his eyes firmly shut. He found himself having difficulty reaching even a simple decision about what to wear.

Uniform or plain clothes?

Uniform gave him the trappings of authority, and lesser ranks were required to salute – the uniform, if not the man – and that was very nice, and gave a warm feeling of being in charge of things.

On the other hand uniform, even the so-called 'summer dress', was uncomfortably hot in the sort of weather forecasted.

Better, from the point of view of creature comfort, to wear a lightweight sports jacket and slacks. Perhaps even a cravat, instead of a tie. Perhaps even sandals instead of shoes. But would that make him look something of a dandy? Something of an elderly idiot? A dandified idiot, perhaps? A man to be scorned? Somebody to be held in contemptuous disrespect?

He lowered his head, shampooed his hair, lathered his body and, all the time, he regretted his words to his wife the previous evening.

## 0630 Hours

Wilf Howes followed the man in the blue track-suit. He did it properly. He did it as he'd seen it done on TV. As he'd seen it done in the films. As he'd read about it being done. Hell's teeth, anybody who didn't know how to 'tail' somebody these days must have been living in a cave all his life.

Mr Le Carré, Mr Deighton and Mr Forsyth had all written reams about the craft. Unless it's a long road, stay a full street behind. If he's on the offside pavement, you stay on the nearside pavement. Keep him in view as much as possible, but never actually look at him. Anticipate any move he might be going to make.

Howes had duly 'anticipated'.

He'd used his walkie-talkie to pass information back to Grafton in the DHQ Telecommunications Room.

'One-nine-nine Howes, here. I have a message. Over.'

'Go ahead.'

'I'm following a man in a blue jogging outfit. I think he's making for B Beat.'

'So?'

'Sergeant Blythe wants him checking out.'

'Why?'

'I don't know why. Ask Blythe.'

'He isn't here. He's out on the streets somewhere.'

'Look! I mean, *look* . . . ' Howes started to gabble. 'Don't – I mean, don't ask *me*. The Sergeant, y'know, the Sergeant gives instructions, and that's it. You don't argue. You don't ask. You shouldn't argue. Just do it. And he's definitely moving towards B Beat. Just, y'know, just tell Fairclough to be ready to take over.'

And now the man in the blue track-suit crossed the road and, in doing so, moved from A Beat to B Beat. There was an arcade of shops and Howes dodged into a narrow side street to watch. As the man in the blue track-suit continued on his way, Police Constable 729 Fairclough stepped from the doorway of Marks and Spencer and followed at a discreet distance.

Howes smiled his appreciation. It was, he thought, very much like the stories told by Mr Le Carré, Mr Deighton and Mr Forsyth . . . but of course this time it was for real.

Section Police Sergeant Blythe was a man who knew his own limitations. He knew he was no genius. He knew he was no hero. On the other hand he also knew he was a good, practical copper, a fair-to-moderate police sergeant who didn't like throwing his weight around, a guy who believed in moderation in all things and an officer who rarely cranked himself up because of the inhumanities he was obliged to witness while on duty.

A nice enough chap, not given to panic and, to a large degree, shock-proof.

But as he rounded the corner at the back of the bungalow he was shocked. The involuntary 'Christ Almighty!' preluded a great intake of breath, followed by a panting, as if he'd just run a great distance. A natural instinct for self-preservation made him stand with his back hard against the brickwork of the bungalow as he stared at what had once been Police Constable Walker.

Walker was dead . . . there was not a shadow of a doubt about *that*.

The body sprawled across the rear doorstep, half in and half out of the bungalow. The helmet had fallen off and had rolled a yard or so down the path. The shirt, the tie and the front of the tunic were all soaked in blood, and blood had spilled onto the step and onto the surface of the concrete path. Pools of the stuff. *Lakes* of it. The marvel was that one human body could once have held so much blood.

The blood came from – and was still coming from – a slit throat, a gash that had opened a gaping mouth of flesh which stretched from hinge to hinge of the jaw. The eyes were staring, out of focus, but in some strange way pleadingly, into eternity.

Blythe was not a fainting man. Never before, in all his life, had he passed out. But he almost did now. He felt the pressure in his ears. The outer edges of his vision blurred a little, and quite suddenly his legs began to tremble.

He blinked his eyes, clenched his fists and sucked in

21

three long, deep breaths of air. His world steadied. Very cautiously – almost unwillingly – he moved towards his dead colleague.

'Don't you come closer, man.'

The voice came from beyond the open door. It was a voice slightly flawed, because it was obviously pitched higher than it should have been, and fear and panic were the striae knocking it off-key.

The voice continued, 'You want the same, man? That's okay by me.'

Blythe tried not to sound scared. He forced himself to speak slowly and deliberately. 'I can't just walk away, squire. You know that. Whoever you are, you know—'

'It makes no matter who I am, man. That ain't no business of yours. Just you listen good. You don't try to be no hero, and make me do something foolish.'

'You've already done something foolish.'

Mentally Blythe was cursing himself. Like so many coppers these days, he didn't automatically carry staff and handcuffs. He took them from their drawer at home and carried them only when he knew they might be needed. The old-time Appointments Parade was now a thing of near-ancient memory but, by God, in those days you *had* to produce a truncheon and a set of handcuffs before you hit the streets. But not these days. These days it was a very individual choice. And, right now, he (along with a lot of other officers) had made a very wrong choice.

He said, 'I'll have to check that he's dead.'

'He's dead, man. You crazy?'

'We don't know for sure.'

'All that juice. Man, he is *dead*.'

'I have to check, squire,' insisted Blythe. 'It's a million-to-one shot, but he might not be.'

'You crazy?' The question wasn't far from a sob.

'I have to check.'

22

He waited for a moment then, when there was no reply, Blythe moved slowly and cautiously towards the body. He didn't look into the darkness of the passage beyond the open door – he might have been too scared to look – but instead he kept his eyes fixed on the savaged body of the constable. Then he knelt down in the pool of blood alongside the body.

He felt the warm stickiness of the blood on his fingers as he made believe he was feeling at the wrist for a pulse while, with the other hand, he gently patted the right trouser-pocket to check whether Walker had come on duty complete with truncheon. The truncheon pocket was empty and Blythe almost sighed with relief. It meant he was relieved of the task of surreptitiously removing a truncheon from the soaked trousers.

The voice said, 'He's dead . . . right?'

'Yes. He's dead,' breathed Blythe.

'Now you know, man, eh? I ain't playing no games.'

'No games,' said Blythe heavily.

'You don't try anything, right? You try anything, you know what to expect.'

'I can't just leave,' said Blythe gently.

'Don't you try anything!'

Blythe nodded, then, very slowly, he rose to his feet. Still not looking into the gloom beyond the open door, he moved to a position near to – alongside – that door, and stood with his back to the wall. He unhooked his personal radio from his tunic and pressed the transmit button. The mouthpiece was less than an inch from his lips as he spoke.

'The man you've just killed is called Walker. Police Constable Walker.'

'I should care what his stinking name is.'

'My name is Blythe. Police Sergeant Blythe. That's how things stand at the moment . . . whoever you are.'

'Who I am ain't important, man. Just that you'd better

23

believe I ain't staying here.'

'You're staying there.' Blythe's finger was hard upon the transmit button. 'Number Twenty-Six, Audsley Avenue. That's where you are. And *that* is where you're staying. Twenty-Six Audsley Avenue.'

'You crazy?'

'Not as crazy as you are, if you think you can walk away from murder.'

Police Constable 943 Charlie Daniels unlaced his shoes, then eased the knot of his tie. He leaned back into the comfort of an armchair, lifted a pint mug of hot, sweet tea from a side table and enjoyed a deep draught. He watched his wife, Beth, and wondered why the hell he hadn't tumbled to the truth long ago.

Beth smiled down at him and asked, 'Do you want a bite to eat, luv?'

'No.'

'A slice of toast?'

'Nothing.'

'You usually do.'

'Not this time.'

She looked a little puzzled but didn't press things.

He swigged more tea, then said, 'I called at the garage.'

'Oh, aye?'

She lowered herself into the companion armchair, a hearthrug's length away.

'I – er . . . ' Daniels cleared his throat, then said, 'I don't like the idea.'

'What idea's that, then?'

She was wearing a blue candlewick dressing-gown. It had fallen open below the sash when she'd sat down. She did nothing to hide the fact that the dressing-gown was the only thing she was wearing.

Daniels said, 'The garage idea.'

'What about it?'

'I don't like it.'

'How d'you mean?' Her eyes widened.

'What I say. I've decided. It's not a good idea.'

'Nay, damn . . . we've agreed.'

'*You've* agreed. You and Chris. Not me.'

'Be hanged for a tale!' Anger and worry mixed in her glare, and her inability to control herself quite as much as he could annoyed Daniels slightly. It was a weakness. One more weakness. One more to be added to the many he'd already discovered. A pretty face, a quite beautiful figure, plus the morals of an alley cat. She snapped, 'You can't play ducks and drakes, y'know. Not like this.'

'Oh, yes.'

'Of all the—'

'Chris can look after himself. He always has done.'

'You're getting at something, aren't you?'

'Of course. I'm getting at you and the nasty little games you play.'

'And what's *that* supposed to mean?'

'Beth . . . ' His voice was strained and weary as he spoke her name. He rubbed the back of his hand across his lips, raised the mug, then lowered it and said, 'Not tea.'

'Eh?'

'I think whisky is more appropriate.'

'You *what*?'

'To drink a health to a new understanding.'

'I don't know what—'

'I'll get it.'

He pushed himself up from the armchair and, a little stiff-legged, walked to the sideboard at the back of the room. He opened one of the side-cupboards and took out a freshly opened bottle of whisky and a glass. He filled the glass, re-stoppered the whisky, then returned to the armchair.

25

Beth Daniels watched him without speaking then, as he once more settled into the armchair, sneered, 'Whisky? And neat? *And* at this time in the morning. You must have money to burn.'

'I shall not be spending much.' He tasted the whisky, then added, 'And when you've left . . .'

'What's that mean?'

'I called at the garage on the way home.'

'So?'

'The owner – the chap we were going to buy it from – was there.'

'So?' Her eyes narrowed slightly.

'Our kid – our Chris – had called earlier this morning.'

She said nothing.

'I know Chris,' he mused. 'He likes his bed. It's Sunday. He isn't working today. He wouldn't have been up and about at this time . . . not normally.'

'Maybe . . . ' She moistened her lips. 'Maybe he's – y'know – maybe he's—'

'*Shut it!*' Daniels allowed his fury to surface for a moment, and she jerked her head back slightly, as if his exclamation had had physical force. Then in a quieter voice he said, '*He's* up and about. *You're* up and about. *I'm* up and about. And it's Sunday. Unusual. Almost unique. *I've* been on duty.' He paused, then ended, 'I won't ask where you and Chris have been.'

'Charlie,' she said hoarsely.

'That's my name.'

'You'll – you'll not believe me, but—'

'I'll not believe you,' he agreed. 'Not this time.'

She took a deep breath, then muttered, 'He – he *made* me.'

'Made you?'

'He came in, late last night. He was drunk. I was scared.'

26

'No.' He shook his head, then threw some whisky down his throat. He said, 'He had you first. Remember? You were shop-soiled when I took over. And nobody ever made you do anything. But – y'know – I was crazy enough to have certain dreams.'

Again Daniels paused. This time he merely moistened his lips from the glass. His tone became bitter as he continued.

'A nice thought, eh? All living together under one roof. No wonder you were both so eager to sell me the con. And I almost bought it. If I hadn't called at the garage this morning. If the owner hadn't mentioned Chris. If you hadn't been up and about when I arrived home. That's how near. That's how *bloody* near!'

'You'll – you'll not believe anything else?' There was, perhaps, a hint of pleading in the question.

'I'd be a fool.'

'If I told you I was sorry.'

'Sorry for what? For having been caught? Sorry that I've at last come up for air?'

'I'll – I'll not leave.'

'One of us will.' Again he tasted the whisky. 'Nine o'clock. A couple of hours from now. If you don't go, *I* go. And if *I* go, you'll have whatever money you have in your purse. No more. Ever.'

She was very dainty. She was tippy-tap-tapping on the concrete of the dog compound, like a four-footed ballerina. She gazed at Police Constable Vine with puzzled, innocent eyes and, although Vine's returned gaze was almost equally puzzled, it held little or no innocence.

'We don't even know your name,' he grumbled. 'And as for me, I'm buggered if I know what you eat. Other than sugar lumps . . . and you're not having any of them.'

Vine turned his back on the compound and returned to the police station. He walked into the Main Office and saw that Grafton was at the switchboard.

Vine said, 'Donkeys. What do they eat?'

Grafton gave the impression of not having heard the question. He was scowling at the switchboard, as if undecided whether to use it or not.

'That donkey in the back,' insisted Vine. 'What the hell do we feed it with? Dog biscuits?'

Again, Grafton didn't seem to hear. Instead, he apparently reached a decision, picked up the handset and began to dial a number.

## 0645 Hours

Four Town Beats. A Beat – the 'Promenade Beat', the beat with the hotels and the class restaurants. D Beat – the 'Residential Beat', the beat with flats and bungalows, the farthest beat from the front. And, sandwiched between A and D Beats, B and C Beats. B Beat had a preponderance of guest houses. C Beat was heavy with lock-up shops and tiny cafés.

And at the top and bottom of A, B, C and D Beats were the two section 'Outside Beats'. North Beat and South Beat. Beats policed by officers not required to report 'on duty' at Rogate-on-Sands Police Station. Beats which stretched from the shore line to the section boundary.

North Beat and South Beat each had its own 'village bobby'; a man of above-average experience, a reliable, street-wise copper who was expected to patrol his personal patch for his own chosen eight hours each day and, at the same time, be willing to come 'on duty' at any hour of the twenty-four when necessary.

Jim Tidy, Police Constable 1122, was the 'Outside

28

Man' responsible for North Beat.

Tidy was glancing through the headlines of the newly delivered local newspaper, waiting for the kettle to boil for the first brew-up of the day, when the telephone bell shattered the early morning quiet.

As he ambled into the hall of his cottage, the thought struck him that police telephones all seemed to be cursed with a particularly loud and vibrant bell which, in turn, was tuned to a remarkably off-key pitch.

He picked the receiver from its rest, and said, 'Police Constable Tidy.'

'Jim.' Tidy recognised Grafton's voice and picked out the worry in his tone. 'It's Grafton here. I've just had a message on the air waves. Walkie-talkie. I think it was from Blythe, and I think he's in trouble.'

'Blythe?'

'He's out on the street with Johnny Walker and – if it *was* Blythe – he was saying something about Walker having been killed.'

'Blythe said that?'

'I *think*. He sort of half identified himself, but radio procedure was all to hell.'

'Did you call back?'

'I tried, but no joy. No response. Just transmit . . . then nothing. I'm a bit worried, Jim.'

'I'm on duty at seven,' volunteered Tidy.

'I know. I just wondered.'

'He's out on D Beat?'

'Audsley Avenue. Number Twenty-Six. That's what came over.'

'From Blythe?'

'I think it was Blythe.' There was a pause, then Grafton said, 'It's a puzzler, Jim. I don't want to panic at nothing . . . but it could be serious. And you have wheels.'

'Leave it to me. I'll be in touch.'

29

Tidy dropped the receiver back onto its rest. He walked into the kitchen to switch off the kettle, then stepped into the lounge to collect his tunic. He buttoned the tunic as he closed the front door of the cottage and walked towards the parked van.

The truth was, Tidy was pleased to have something to do. Just himself, alone in the house, was pretty rough. In the mornings especially. To awaken and not be alongside Madge underlined the magnitude of his loss. The rest – the doing of his own housework, the making of his own meals, the washing of his own clothes – wasn't too bad. It kept him busy and kept his mind occupied. It made sure he was tired, and the hot toddy before he crawled into bed made sure he slept.

But when he awoke . . . that was when he *really* knew what had happened.

He climbed into the van, turned the ignition key and steered the vehicle from its hard standing onto the road.

She'd liked living here at Finehead, the tiny hamlet on the outskirts of Rogate-on-Sands. Countryside, with fresh sea air. Less than two miles from the coast – to the bay, to the beach, to the stretch of sand as clean as a new pin, a stretch of sand few people not living in the immediate vicinity even knew about. She'd loved that beach. Lazing in the sun. Walking by the water's edge in the late summer evening. Or maybe wandering the lanes, blackberrying. She'd been so happy . . . so many times.

'Y'know, Jim, we're lucky.' She'd said it often.

'We're lucky,' he'd agreed. But it had been an empty, throw-away agreement and, although he hadn't known it, or even meant it to be, at the time it had lacked the deep-down sincerity he now wished he'd injected into the remark.

She'd said, 'I think this must be one of the nicest beats

30

in the country.'

'It's nice.'

'And I'm so glad you're a policeman.'

And she'd meant that, too. To her, being a copper's wife had given their marriage an extra fillip. It was what she'd believed, and no amount of disappointments had altered that belief. Her man's job was law-enforcement. He commanded respect ... and being her man was reason enough for earning that respect.

The string of large houses, standing in their own immaculately tended gardens, was proof that he'd reached the outskirts of Rogate-on-Sands, that he was moving into D Beat, therefore, instead of driving instinctively, while thoughts played tag with memories in his skull, Tidy concentrated on making his way towards Audsley Avenue.

Police Constable 729 Fairclough couldn't quite figure out how he'd lost the man in the blue track-suit. Indeed, he couldn't figure out how he'd lost them both, the man and his great, sloppy dog. They'd disappeared. Vanished without trace. There one minute. The next minute ... nothing. Slowly and carefully Fairclough retraced his steps. Back along Whinnley Lane, then right and into Claypit Drive. They'd been there when he (Harry Fairclough) had turned into Whinnley Lane. He'd seen them. Just a fleeting glimpse but quite clearly, before they'd turned right into Vallance Crescent. But then, when he'd reached the corner ... emptiness.

Of course it *had* to be Vallance Crescent. A stretch of thoroughfare with half-a-dozen mock-Victorian shopping arcades leading off its not inconsiderable length. Narrow, winding tunnels of shop windows, each used as a short cut to the car park, or to Avenue Lane or to Peelslade. Or, come to that, to *anywhere*.

31

But having said that – having admitted the possibility – the fact remained that Mister Blue Track-Suit (and his bloody great dog) must have sent sparks flying from their heels. They must have moved with considerable speed, otherwise Fairclough must have seen them.

Which suggested that Blue Track-Suit had tumbled to the fact that he was being followed. Which, in turn, suggested that he had some objection to being followed. Which could mean he was up to no good.

Fairclough scowled and muttered, 'Where are you, you bloody man? Where the hell are you?'

To be on the safe side, he began to check every door and window before turning into the first shopping arcade, to verify that nobody – especially a 'nobody' wearing a blue track-suit, and with a daft, setter-type dog – was doing things they shouldn't be doing.


## 0700 Hours

Blythe wasn't too far from blind panic, and was honest enough to know it. The trembling of his legs couldn't be controlled. He clenched his fists, leaned hard against the brickwork of the side of the bungalow and took deep breaths, but nothing seemed to help. He was shaking, and he was shaking because of shock. And he recognised this, too.

The thing – the thing that, minutes before, had been Johnny Walker – sprawling and still spilling red across the step, was something of which nightmares are made. Sudden deaths, fatal accidents, suicides, blood, shit and brains . . . sure, he'd seen his share of those things at various times in his service. But this was different, and one of the differences was that he hadn't been 'called out'. He hadn't 'attended'. He hadn't had time to ready himself for what he might see. That, plus the fact that 'it' had been a friend, alive, walking alongside him and holding a conversation only moments before.

Reinforcements were needed, and he hoped to God Grafton had had the simple gumption to interpret what he'd tried to say. On the other hand, maybe he shouldn't have given a damn; maybe he should have bawled for assistance, and the hell with whether the madman in the bungalow heard or not. Maybe that would have been the wise way. But at the time it hadn't seemed so.

The killer was listening. The killer could hear every word. And whoever the bastard was who'd sliced up Johnny Walker, Blythe wanted him there, inside the bungalow, until assistance arrived. The animal mustn't be allowed to make a run for it; he mustn't be scared into taking off and losing himself in the soon-to-be-available holiday crowds.

This fear, this possibility that Walker's killer might hear something which would make him scared enough to run, had been Blythe's reason for not following standard radio procedure. It was why, after sending his half-hearted message, he'd immediately switched the radio to 'off'. He hadn't wanted to remind the killer that coppers had personal radios.

As if to emphasise that thought, Blythe unclipped the set from his tunic and placed it on the path alongside his feet. As he straightened, he pulled a handkerchief from his trouser pocket. The intention had been to wipe his sweat-soaked face, but as he raised the handkerchief he saw the stain already made on the linen by the blood on his fingers, and instead he started to wipe his hands.

'Oh, for Christ's sake!' he breathed. 'For *Christ's* sake!'

He shuddered, opened his fingers and allowed the soiled handkerchief to fall onto the path. He bent his head back and rested the top of his skull against the brickwork. He gulped in cool, refreshing air. Gradually

33

– very gradually – some degree of control returned. The panic became a little less blind.

After a few moments he turned away from the wall and called, 'I think you'd be wise to give yourself up . . . whoever you are.'

'You crazy?'

'You're in trouble already. I don't have to tell you that.'

'Shut it, man!'

'Don't make things worse.'

'Like I say, don't you try to be no hero, copper. I ain't no fool. I can't get into more trouble. Just you remember that. I ain't got nothing to lose.'

'I can say you co-operated.'

'You stupid?'

'It might help.'

'Don't you bull me, man.' There was a strange impatience in the tone.

'I can—'

'Cut it, man! Zip it!' The words were almost shouted, and the tone was moving up the scale towards a scream. Then in the previous, impatient voice, 'I'm thinking, copper. Don't you try stop me from thinking.'

Vic Wood was moving quietly towards Pension Day. No ripples, no wash, no waves. Less than three more years and he was free-wheeling, and he was ready to admit it to anybody curious enough to enquire. In all his service he'd torn up no trees. Not once had he bothered to make his mark. He'd had a nice, steady, come-day-go-day career, which was how he'd always wanted it. His ambition was to draw a pension for at least as long as he'd accepted a police salary and eventually, and at a date away and gone to hell in the future, be able to meet his maker and proudly boast that he'd licked the system; that he'd put very little into the pot, but taken a hell of a lot out.

34

Wood had worked C Beat for almost ten years. He knew every shop, every café, every club and every boozer on the beat. He knew a hundred-and-one places where he could shelter, unseen, from bad weather. He knew another hundred-and-one places where he could be fed buckshee tea and cakes. He knew a third hundred-and-one places where people would happily swear they'd seen him passing, and had called him in for a spot of legal advice.

Vic Wood had trained C Beat to sit up and take peanuts.

He was saying, 'Not like it used to be, eh? Not like it was in the old days.'

'No beat any more. No section work.'

The man agreeing with Wood was elderly and fat and running to seed. Wood didn't know – and, had he known, he wouldn't have cared – that all tenor sax men tend to look fat and as if they were running to seed. It is perhaps something to do with the rich, round notes they blow from their instruments. The man had sad eyes and a doleful expression . . . as if the jazz, which was the touchstone of his life, had all been firmly anchored in a minor key.

He said, 'It's all fancy shell piano playing these days. No stride. All small combo stuff. All twee. No Basie.'

'Not like the old days,' repeated Wood.

'Who the hell plays like Vido Musso today? Who blows as solid as Herschel Evans?'

'Who indeed?'

'I blame Stan Getz,' bemoaned the elderly musician.

'Getz,' agreed Wood, who in truth had never before heard the name and, if asked, wouldn't have known how to spell it.

'He blows for Kenton, he blows for Herman . . . then he goes bananas.'

'Bananas,' echoed Wood.

35

'Copenhagen has a lot to answer for.'

'I hate the guy,' offered Wood.

'Eh?'

'Copenhagen. He could never play. Not for nuts.'

'Copenhagen?' The musician stared.

'Oh! Y'mean Copenhagen?'

'What else?'

'I thought you meant . . .'

'The Café Montmartre. That's what I mean.'

'Oh yeah. Sure.' Wood grabbed at the runaway conversation and rescued what little he could. He grinned and said, 'Cross-purposes. It happens sometimes. I have things on my mind.'

They were in a tiny box-room at the rear of a newsagent's shop. While they talked, they sipped at mugs of freshly brewed tea and nibbled at chocolate bars. Beyond the box-room, in the body of the shop, the proprietor – the musician's son – was sorting newspapers with practised speed and arranging them in bundles for delivery boys and girls who had not yet arrived. The visit of Police Constable Wood was a regular occurrence when he was on early shift. The newsagent didn't mind. It kept his father busy, yarning about the old and long-dead days, and away from the newspapers. It stopped him from screwing up the sorting and prevented them both starting the day with a great argument.

The elderly musician said, 'The big bands don't swing any more. It's all James Last stuff. Showman stuff. No drive. No real beat.'

'I like beat,' said Wood. He sipped at his tea noisily. 'I like a good drummer myself.'

'Drummers who know their stuff.'

'Of course.'

'Who know their place in the band.'

'For sure.'

36

'Not front men.'

'No . . . never front men.'

'Buddy Rich had a lot to answer for.'

'You can say that again.'

'When he was with Dorsey, fine. When he was with Shaw, fine. But he got too fancy. That's when he went wrong.'

'He shouldn't have turned so fancy,' agreed Wood.

'Good days, though.' The musician almost smiled.

'I'll say.'

'The timing. The rests. The attack. The section work. Horns and reeds, passing the melody around. "Talking" to each other. They don't do it these days. Maybe they can't. Maybe they're too damned dumb. And that wouldn't surprise me too much, either.'

Vine's considered opinion of Rogate-on-Sands Police Station was that it was a prolonged and permanent pain in the neck. It was a do-it-yourself shunt-up, and the sort of working environment calculated to bring on ulcers, grey hairs and heart attacks.

Vine – Police Constable 221 Henry Vine – had that ridiculously doleful look of the late Buster Keaton. But there was a difference; with Keaton it was a carefully rehearsed act, meant to emphasise a unique comic genius. With Vine, it was for real. With Keaton, it made people laugh; with Vine, it made people cross.

'Why?' asked Grafton irritably. 'Why can't you come up with just one piece of reasonably constructive criticism?'

'I'm not paid to have brainwaves.' Vine's brow furrowed into slightly deeper folds. 'I'm paid to do a job. I'm told what to do . . . I do it.'

'Like – at this moment – feeding prisoners?'

'Just that.'

'One single, solitary prisoner?'

37

'I haven't checked, but that's what I'm told. And one donkey.'

'One basic breakfast?'

'He's not getting two. Lay money on it.'

'Boy!' Grafton blew out his cheeks. 'Don't come out in spots from overwork.'

'Lay money on *that*, too.'

'Why won't you nip along to Audsley Avenue? Check out that things are okay?'

'And if the prisoner snuffs it?'

'Hell's teeth! That's not likely to —'

'But if he does?'

'All right. But you, sitting on your fat arse here in the nick, won't make him immortal.'

'I'm where I should be.'

'So?'

'I'm where I was told to be. I'm obeying orders.'

'Okay.' Grafton sounded a little desperate. 'Let's tool around with some more stupid ideas and assume Barstow's dead already. That he's snuffed it within the last few minutes. What then? How does that fit in with your I'm-all-right-Jack ideas?'

'So he's dead,' intoned Vine expressionlessly. 'After I've checked the circulars, I'll take his breakfast to the cell. If he happens to be some undertaker's profit, that's not my fault. He's stiff. Just don't ask me to subscribe to a wreath.'

'All right,' pleaded Grafton. 'Sit here at the switchboard. Let me go round to Audsley Avenue.'

'*Me*? Take on *your* job?'

'Yeah.'

'As well as my own?'

'It wouldn't cripple you. It wouldn't—'

'Grafton, there's one thing they never do in this crummy force. They don't overstaff.'

'I'm not asking—'

'They wouldn't put a man on switchboard and a man on cells if there was a cat-in-hell's chance of one man being able to do both jobs. They've already worked things out. They know better than you – better than me – how to distribute all available manpower.'

'Don't you *care?*' Grafton stared in near-disbelief.

'I don't give a monkey's,' said Vine flatly. 'That's how things are. How the clowns up top want them to be. I don't go around setting precedents.'

Tidy braked the van to a halt, climbed out and walked up the path leading to the bungalow. He rounded the side of the bungalow, then stopped as if he'd hit a brick wall.

He breathed, 'Holy cow!'

'Thank God!' Blythe looked up. For a split second something approximating a quick smile of sheer relief touched his lips. Then he said, 'Grafton must have understood.'

Tidy nodded. His eyes remained on the mutilated body of Walker. 'Whoever did this, is he still inside?'

'Yes.'

'What about the front door? Can't he—'

'He hasn't tried. Not yet.'

'How many are there?'

'Just the one, I think. I *think*. I'm damned if I know.'

'Have you contacted him?'

'Yes.'

'Spoken to him?'

'Yes. He's threatened to do the same to anybody who tries to get inside.'

Tidy compressed his lips.

Blythe added, 'I think he means it.'

'Why not? What has he to lose?' Tidy nodded slowly. For the first time he looked closely at Blythe's shock-shattered expression. Then he said, 'Hang on,

39

Joe. Just stand here. don't try to *do* anything. I'll cover the front door and I'll blow the whistle for more troops.'

'Thanks.' Blythe allowed his chin to drop onto his chest for a moment, then he repeated, 'Thanks.'

The town was stretching itself after a good night's sleep. There was a gradual awakening; a busy stopping and starting of milk-delivery vans; a silent streaming of bicycles ridden by men and women who, Sunday or weekday, had early morning work to go to. It was Rogate-on-Sands. It was a holiday town, and it was a time in the thick of the holiday period. Staff from the hotels – workers who lived out, either in their own homes or in digs – hurried along the pavements; the kitchen helps, the waiters and waitresses, the bedroom cleaners, the general fetchers and carriers; so many people needed to ensure the comfort and well-being of little more than their number.

Many of the shops were opening. The attendant was unlocking the gates of the pier. Another attendant lifted down the shutters protecting the window of the sea-front, municipal car park office. Things were definitely moving.

The tide had turned and the sea's edge was slowly creeping up the beach towards the base of the promenade. The sun was growing stronger and the shadows darker and more clear-cut.

Some of the elderly citizenry were up and about; the retired men and women whose lives were empty other than with deliberately self-organised habits. To rise early. To enjoy full, careful ablutions. To walk two miles before breakfast. To take an old and reluctant dog for a walk. To drive an electrically-operated wheelchair down to the promenade, along Rock Walk, then back home via the shops. To walk to one of the sea-front shelters, meet a friend, then sit and exchange opinions about

40

what had happened in the world during the last twenty-four hours.

A thousand-and-one carefully worked-out routines with which to fill otherwise empty lives. To work like hell, killing the boredom that comes with the end of a working life.

Sometimes to stop and chat with a passing policeman.

Constable Howes, who didn't understand these things, said, 'Very nice, eh?' His beard moved as he spoke. His cheeks were rosy, his eyes twinkled and he looked even more like a garden gnome. He chattered, 'Y'know – I mean – yes, retirement must be very nice.'

'You think that, do you?'

The questioner was an oldster with a distinctly military bearing. The ramrod back and the clipped moustache were, perhaps, offset by a skull with only a few wispy hairs. Nevertheless, and despite the rubber-ferrule walking stick, there was the hint of impatient authority in the barked rejoinder.

The oldster continued, 'You seriously think retirement is "nice", do you?'

'Well, er, yes. Y'know ... if you have your health. That's what I mean. Not – not if you can't—'

'Balderdash!'

'Oh!'

'Man,' snapped the oldster. 'Man. The only animal stupid enough to stop moving arbitrarily. To cease to function. To "retire".'

'Oh!'

'We are a pack animal, Constable. Didn't you know that? Is that news to you?'

'Er – well – er . . .'

'A pack animal,' repeated the oldster. 'Our natural instinct is to leave the lame and the injured – the old and the useless – to fend for themselves. To die.'

'Ah! Yes. But—'

41

'No "buts". The pack comes first. The pack, as a single entity, has to remain healthy. Whichever parts of it *are* healthy must contribute to the well-being of the pack. No "retiring". We've gone against nature.'

'I say, that's – er – that's a bit . . . I mean, it's not that I'm arguing. Just that – y'know . . .'

'At a given age – at a purely arbitrary age – we are told we are no longer needed. The pack no longer requires us. We're made to "retire". And thoughtless people like you have the gall to call that "nice".'

'No. I mean – y'know – I didn't *mean* to say—'

'We're dismissed from the pack. Regardless of the fact that we're not ill. Not injured. Not useless. Damnation, we can still contribute. We have experience. We've *made* our mistakes. Those of us with sense have learned from them. We could help the pack survive. We could—'

'Excuse me, sir.' Howes lifted his walkie-talkie closer to his ear and listened to the message, then spoke into the mouthpiece. 'Right. I'm on my way.'

The oldster barked, 'D'you want a lift?'

'Well, if you have . . .'

'The car's parked round the corner.' The oldster lifted his walking stick in a vague, pointing gesture. 'And I know where Audsley Avenue is.'

'Oh – er – no. I mean . . . thanks a lot. I mean, yes. That would be a big help. That would . . .'

'For God's sake! Don't just stand there spluttering. If I heard that contraption you were talking into aright, this is something of an emergency.'


## 0715 Hours

Constable Fairclough was half-way down the second shopping arcade – Hamilton Mews – when he heard the sound of running footsteps in the distance. From (or so

42

it seemed) Simpson Mews, which was next to, and parallel with, Hamilton Mews. He paused and turned his head a little, in order to listen more intently, then, having decided the sound *was* coming from Simpson Mews, raced to the end of Hamilton Mews, swerved left, then left again and did a half-racing-skid into the next shopping arcade.

The realisation that he was entering the arcade at the wrong end – that his quarry had already left the arcade at the other end – was immediately offset by the smell of burning and the mist of smoke filling the arcade from the house agent's premises.

Fairclough ran to the door of the office, saw the smoke-filled room and, without hesitation, smashed the sole of his shoe through the glass of the door. He kicked the loose shards free then felt for the latch and the bolts before opening the door and, ignoring a spasm of coughing, began to stamp on the burning rags that had been piled up beneath the letter-box.

There was much smoke but no flames. There was smouldering and, no doubt, there would be charring. It was possible that, had the fire been allowed to build, the premises might have suffered a real blaze but, because it had been caught in time, that wasn't going to happen.

Fairclough shuffled his feet amongst the smouldering rags for a few more moments, then hurried into the back room. He found a sink and, in the sink, a washing-up bowl. A good pressure of water filled the bowl as he fought to control his smoke-impaired breathing, then he hurried back to the front door and dumped the water onto the smoking rags.

He returned to the back room. As he refilled the bowl, he had breath enough to mutter, 'You stupid sods, whoever you are. You stupid, *stupid* sods.'

*

43

The telephone bell shattered his sleep and the Detective Inspector stretched out an arm, lifted the receiver from its rest and mumbled, 'Fuller.'

'Inspector, I think you should know.' Fuller recognised the slightly distorted voice of Constable Grafton. 'I've just had a message from Constable Tidy. Constable Walker's been murdered.'

'Jesus Christ! That's all we need.'

'Sir, I thought I should—'

'Details.' Fuller was suddenly very wide awake. He hoisted himself into a sitting position and continued, 'Where? When?'

'Within the last hour, sir. A stabbing. At Audsley Avenue.'

'Who's there?'

'Tidy and Sergeant Blythe, sir.'

'Superintendent Crosby?'

'No, sir. I've tried to raise him, but Mrs Crosby says he's out on duty.'

'At *this* time?'

'Yes, sir.'

'On a *Sunday*?'

'That's what she says.'

'Try to reach him.'

'I'll try.' Grafton cleared his throat and continued, 'Sir, according to Tidy the murderer's still there.'

'Still where?'

'On the premises, in Audsley Avenue.'

'Right. Get Headquarters.' Fuller swung his feet onto the floor. 'Tell them we need some squad cars at the scene as soon as possible. Then notify Detective Sergeant Wragg. Tell him I'm on my way. I'll meet him there.'

'Yes, sir. I've – er – I've tried to contact some of the men on town duty, but I can't raise them. I'll—'

'Who?'

44

'Constable Wood and Constable Fairclough. It seemed sensible to—'

'Keep trying. And Crosby. If anybody wants me, I'm on my way to the scene.'

'Up there, on the rostrum, there's no such thing as free-wheeling.' The elderly musician was warming to his subject. He knew what he was talking about and he was obviously enjoying passing on his knowledge. 'The mid-thirties Goodman outfit. They were all good section men. The three horn men – James, Griffin and Elman – they led the attack, but the reeds were in there, pumping.'

The truth was, Constable Wood didn't give a monkey's toss. Most of the so-called 'swing bands' gave him a quick bout of indigestion. *His* particular cup of tea was good old-fashioned brass band music. Years back – long before he'd joined the force – Wood had been a junior member of a town band. Not much of a band – nothing 'prize' about it – but at an early age he'd learned to appreciate the art of triple-tonguing. That, of course, had been long before 'pop' had moved into what Wood counted as the tuneless caterwauling that passed as present-day music. Nor had he ever understood the passion with which an older generation than his held giants of the Big Band Era.

The elderly musician's enthusiasms were an acceptable boredom that Wood was prepared to tolerate as the going price for a mug of tea, a chocolate bar and a place in which to hide, away from any possible hassle.

'The reed sections.' The elderly musician leaned forward a little. He used his hands to emphasise what he was saying. 'I figure the best was Basie's 1940 line-up. Young, Washington, Warren and Tate. Although, I dunno . . . ' A faraway look misted his eyes. In a more dreamy voice he continued, 'Gil Rodin could organise a

45

very mean sax group. First with Pollack. Then with Crosby.'

'I didn't know Bing had a—'

'*Bob.*' The elderly musician frowned quick annoyance. 'Bing's brother. Rumour has it he was more of a nuisance than a help, but the band stuck him up front because of his name. When Pollack folded. When he went spare about some female who couldn't sing for toffee. That's when . . . '

The elderly musician's son poked his head around the door jamb and said, 'Should you be on the street, Constable?'

'Aye, eventually.'

'I thought you should know, that's all. There's a flash car just crawled past, with a uniformed bloke driving. Peaked cap. Scrollwork round the neb. Seems to be looking for somebody.'

Constable Tidy gave a tiny nod towards the body of PC Walker and said, 'We can't just leave him there. Not just *leave* him.'

'I know, but . . . ' Blythe rubbed the back of a hand across his dry lips. He breathed, 'I'm sorry.'

'Forget it.'

Jim Tidy knew exactly what Blythe meant. The Sergeant was, indeed, 'sorry', but the two words were more of an explanation than an apology. They were meant to convey a state of mind which, according to all the law-enforcement text books, an experienced police officer should have rid himself of within his first couple of years of service. Thus the theory, but Blythe hadn't rid himself of that state of mind. He was not, therefore, the 'complete copper'. He was still human enough to be shocked, and humane enough to lose complete control, albeit only momentarily.

Tidy glanced at Blythe's face, noticed the smudge of

46

blood where the back of his hand had touched the corner of his mouth, but he was wise enough to remain silent.

Instead, he asked, 'How are we going to do it?'

'If . . . ' Blythe paused and sucked in a deep breath. In a steadier tone he said, 'If I stand astride him. In the doorway. To keep the mad bastard inside away from you. Then, if you can manage to drag him clear. Away from the step. Then – y'know – we'll take things as they come.'

'Fine.' Tidy nodded. He watched Blythe's face then added, 'When you're ready, then.'

'Hang on.' Blythe moved along towards the rear door of the bungalow, then called, 'You in there.'

There was no answer.

Again Blythe called, 'You in there. Can you hear me?'

'Ain't nothing you have to say to me, man.'

'Are you listening?'

'I tell you, man, ain't nothing—'

'Just *listen*!' Blythe's voice held an unaccustomed ring of authority. Then in a quieter, more reasonable tone, 'We're going to move the body of our colleague. Understand? Just that. Nothing more. It isn't a trick. We're just going to move the body.' Blythe paused. When there was no reply, he continued, 'It's quite simple. I'm going to stand on the step. I'm going to —'

'No way, man!'

'Just shut up and listen! I'm not asking, and we're not putting it up for discussion. I'm *telling* you. I'm going to stand on the step. With my back to the door. I'll make no move to come inside. I'll not try to—'

'You better remember that, copper.'

'I'll make no move to come inside,' repeated Blythe, 'but I'll be there. And a constable will help me to move the body. Do you understand all that?'

'You think I'm gonna—'

47

'Yes, I think you are "going to", because you've no choice in the matter. You're "going to", because I'm going to do it anyway. I'm not asking permission. I'm simply explaining what comes next.'

Blythe glanced at Tidy then said, 'Right behind me, Jim. And for Christ's sake don't waste any time.'

There was a split second's hesitation before Blythe stepped away from the wall and over the body of Constable Walker, then mounted the rear step, turned and, with his back to the open door, stood, feet astride the corpse and with his hands raised and gripping the uprights of the wooden door-surround. It was as far as he could bring himself to go; as a human shield, between whoever was inside the bungalow and Tidy.

It was, perhaps, one of the most deliberately courageous acts Blythe had ever performed. It represented the absolute limit of his personal self-control. To turn his back on whoever – whatever – lurked within the gloom of the bungalow, in order that Tidy might drag a dead colleague out of the immediate environs of a sudden nightmare.

He looked ahead, straight ahead. Not right, not left, not up and certainly not down. He stared into the out-of-focus distance at his own eye-level, and tried to shut out the sound and stop his runaway imagination.

He heard the sound of heels being dragged along a parquet floor; the double, muffled thud as the heels dropped to a lower step and then to the path. He heard the soft wheeze of Tidy's heavy breathing. The whispered, 'Come on, my beauty,' as the Constable gave an extra heave.

He heard other sounds, too. Sounds to which he could not put a definite name. Gentle, horrific gurglings. A soft, disgusting bubbling. His mind ran riot; he wanted to shout to Tidy to either hurry or leave the body where it was.

Then, in a slightly off-key tone, Tidy said, 'That's it, then, Sergeant,' and Blythe heard another sound from behind him.

Later, when asked – when questioned – Blythe could not describe the sound. Or indeed whether there had *been* a sound. Whether perhaps it had been one more piece of a whirling imagination. He couldn't be absolutely sure. It might have been instinct. Some 'knowledge' beyond and separate from the normal and understood senses. Nevertheless, his final statement insisted that he had 'heard' something . . . this, for want of a better, less believable explanation.

He turned. His feet and legs became entangled. He fell sideways, then forward and into the doorway of the bungalow. At that instant he was marked for life.

Whether or not the coloured youth would have used the open cut-throat razor might be open to doubt. He'd obviously used it on Walker. He was approaching the toppling Blythe with the razor held high and ready to strike. It is equally true that, as Blythe stumbled towards the youth and tried to regain his balance, the youth gave a sobbing yell of sheer panic and reacted by slashing wildly with the blade.

It cut Blythe diagonally across the face, from above the left eye, across the nose and down across the right cheek. It hit bone but, for a moment, there was no pain. The razor was like a scalpel and the speed of the cut made the wound clean, perfect but terrible.

As Blythe belatedly raised his right hand in an attempt to fend off the blow, the razor continued its downward sweep and sliced through the cloth of the sleeve and the flesh of the forearm. This time it hurt. It felt like being touched with red hot metal and Blythe gave out a yell of pain.

He'd just about regained his balance when Tidy grabbed him by the waist and threw him back onto the path. Tidy continued the movement, grabbed at the door handle and yanked the rear door of the bungalow closed.

'What's happening?' Beth Daniels looked worried. It was a situation she had never before encountered. She expanded the question a little. 'At half-past nine . . . What's happening, Charlie?'

'Did I say half-past?'

'Aye.' She nodded.

'I thought I said nine o'clock.'

'I think you said half-past,' lied Beth.

'What's thirty minutes?' Charlie Daniels smiled. It was a slow smile as if something mildly humorous had touched his imagination. It was a strangely secretive smile. He murmured, 'In a whole lifetime, what's thirty minutes?'

She was suspicious and perhaps a little frightened.

She asked, 'What are you getting at?'

'An observation,' he smiled. 'That a mere thirty minutes isn't really very long.'

'What are you going to do?'

'You'll be the first to know.'

And now she was worried, and it showed in her tone. She was worried because, for the first time, she'd lost control. Emotionally she was in a strange land and she was blind. She knew, instinctively, that this time her husband wasn't going to be manipulated. His quiet, ice-cold certainty was something she'd never encountered before. His attitude reflected a complete lack of emotion; and this from a man whose depressions and enthusiasms she'd learned to control and channel to her own ends.

'What are you going to do?' she repeated. 'Come nine, or whatever time you have in mind, what happens?'

'One of us leaves.' Daniels re-corked the whisky bottle

50

and placed it by his chair – alongside the now empty glass – then continued, 'That's what happens. No fuss. No palaver. Either you go or I go.'

'Where – where can *I* go?' She was trying the little-girl-lost routine. It had worked before, but this time it was getting her nowhere. She tried harder. Her face crumpled, but the fact that she couldn't cry at will did nothing to help. She whined, 'I've nothing and nobody without you.'

'Oh, come *on.*' Daniels allowed a quick, contemptuous grin to touch his lips.

'I'd be lost. Who'd – y'know – who'd look after me?'

'Chris,' he suggested.

'That's – that's—'

'Beth, tonight wasn't the first time.' He made it a bald statement of fact, not a question.

'I – I – y'know . . . ' Gradually, skilfully, she changed tack. She moved from the heartbroken-child routine to one of the okay-we're-both-adults-let's-face-things-and-behave-in-an-adult-manner ploys. She said, 'I could make it the last time. Very easily, if that's what you want.'

'There shouldn't have been a first time,' sighed Daniels.

'But – y'know – never again.'

'Until the next time you're found out,' he mocked gently.

'There won't *be* a—'

'Oh, for God's sake!' His impatience surfaced for a moment. 'Until the next time one of you becomes too sure. Until the next time you're careless.'

'There won't *be* a next time.'

'Not with me. That's for sure,' he agreed.

'We're still man and wife,' she argued. The tone was as desperate as the argument. 'We're still married.'

'We have a piece of paper. We spoke certain words.

51

We both agreed to some basic rules. But you've broken those rules, so I'm making some new rules, and one of them is that one of us leaves this house by nine o'clock. Nine-thirty at the latest.'

'If you seriously think *I'm* leaving—'

'It's your choice. If you stay, you'll have the house. You'll have the furniture. You'll have what money you have in your purse. You'll also have the mortgage. But it's your choice. Just make it, that's all.'

The car drew to a halt. It was not one of those tyre-burning, high-screaming halts beloved of television and cinematograph tale-spinners, but the car *had* been travelling at speed and the brakes *had* been applied with a certain savagery, therefore Police Constable 199 Howes was subjected to an unexpected jerk before he was able to unclip the seat belt, open the door and duck out onto the pavement. The oldster could move for his age and by the time Howes was hurrying up the garden path the two men were moving neck-and-neck.

They rounded the front corner of the bungalow, then the rear corner, and then they both did a little waltz as they stopped, almost lost their footing and grabbed each other to steady themselves.

Howes' eyes widened and he gabbled, 'What . . .?' He gulped in breath, and tried again. 'Oh, my God! Jim, what the hell's . . .?'

The short stretch of path between the corner and the rear door seemed to be awash with blood. A flash thought entered then left Howes' mind. That he must be asleep; that this must be a particularly nasty nightmare. Then he knew it was no dream, and the words came tumbling from his mouth.

The oldster pushed past him and rapped, 'Constable, who have you sent for?'

'Help.' Tidy was kneeling alongside the sobbing

Blythe, holding a soaked, folded handkerchief against the slashed face. 'I've sent for help. I've been onto—'

'Specifically?'

'I've – I've—'

'An ambulance? Have you sent for an ambulance?'

'Not specifically. But—'

'You, Constable.' The oldster turned to Howes. 'Use that wireless-set contraption of yours. We want an ambulance. *Tell* them, don't *ask*. Urgently.' He returned his attention to Tidy and said, 'You need something bigger than that to hold against his face. And press it hard! And keep his head up. Try to prevent him swallowing too much blood.'

## *0730 Hours*

Fairclough was almost sure he'd managed to douse the fire. *Almost* sure, but fires were a little like sudden deaths. Coppers weren't allowed to decide officially whether a stiff *was* a stiff. No arms, no legs, no head – it didn't matter a damn, no dumb flatfoot was ever allowed to reach a very obvious conclusion. It needed a medic. And it didn't matter how shiny and new the medic was. And never mind how many stiffs the copper had handled throughout a long and gory police career. It still needed the medic to pronounce 'Life extinct'.

As with stiffs, so with fires. The Fire Service reserved the sole right to decide whether or not a fire had been properly extinguished.

Therefore, follow the Rule Book. Don't make too many waves. Send for the Fire Service, complete with tender and men in oilskins, and let *them* poke around in the debris, then state the obvious. And why not?

Fairclough sighed and hurried from Simpson Mews. When he reached the street he pressed the transmition button on his walkie-talkie and said, 'B Beat to Control. Fairclough here. Can you contact the—'

'Get off the air, Fairclough.' Despite the metallic distortion, Grafton's voice sounded tight and angry.

'Hey, listen. I want—'

'I don't give a damn *what* you want.'

'What the hell—'

'I've been wanting *you* since forever, but you haven't seen fit to —'

'I've been in a dead area. In Simpson Mews. I'm reporting a—'

'*Get off the air, Fairclough!* All hell's boiling up in Audsley Avenue. I'm trying to contact some of the gold braid.'

'I want the Fire Service.'

'You want *nothing* until I've fixed things for Audsley Avenue.'

'Can I quote that?'

'You can quote just what the hell you like. Just get off the air.'


It was moving up the face towards eight o'clock and, gradually, the first Sunday newspaper delivery was coming to an end. The delivery man working Audsley Avenue paused at the gate of Number Twenty-Six and stared up the path. Something was 'up'. From the rear of the bungalow came faint sounds of activity. And there shouldn't *be* activity, because Arkwright had cancelled his newspaper delivery until a week next Monday. Not *next* Monday – a *week* next Monday.

A police constable darted from the rear of the bungalow.

'Excuse me.' The delivery man raised a hand in a gentle, attention-attracting gesture.

'Yes?' Howes looked both flustered and annoyed.

'There shouldn't – I mean, there's nobody at home. Is there?'

'Yes – I mean, *no*. I don't know. Why?'

'There shouldn't be. Not today. That's why I asked. Because there shouldn't be.'

'That's all right, then.'

'Eh?'

'All right,' repeated Howes. 'If there shouldn't be anybody at home. There *isn't* anybody at home. Everything's as it should be.'

Howes' white beard bobbed and wagged as he talked and the impression was of a man merely making noises but not actually saying anything.

'Is everything all right?' asked the delivery man.

'Why – why shouldn't it be?'

'Just that – y'know . . .'

'No. I don't know.' Howes swallowed. 'Go away. There's nothing here for you. Just go away.'

'Yes. All right. Sorry.'

With some reluctance the delivery man walked away.

Howes heard the distant sound of an ambulance siren growing louder. He looked up Audsley Avenue and saw Fuller's car approaching. He blew out his cheeks and closed his eyes in relief. Things weren't so lonely any more. The back-up was arriving. From here on, all he had to do was obey orders.

Meanwhile, the delivery man turned a corner and headed for a telephone kiosk. It was something he and a couple of his buddies in Rogate-on-Sands did for Tom Tolby, the Number One reporter on the local newsrag. Tolby was also the resident stringer for a quartet of nationals, and the tip-off link for local TV and radio stations.

Telling Tolby anything was like dropping a fair-sized stone into still water; the ripples multiplied and spread out from the centre.

55

Not that the delivery man was paid anything for the information. It gave him a temporary feeling of power and (maybe) next time they met in some pub, Tolby would pay for an extra round of drinks. No more than that but, human nature being what it was, that was enough.

Fairclough felt hard done by. He'd extinguished the fire. Fire Service or not, he *had* extinguished the fire.

That being so, he *might* have saved the whole of the house agent's premises from being gutted. Maybe the whole of Simpson Mews. Indeed, maybe . . .

Fairclough slammed the brakes on personal day-dreams, and ruefully admitted to himself that it hadn't been much of a fire in the first place. Little more than a smouldering job.

Nevertheless . . .

Credit where due. He it was who'd spotted the fire. He it was who'd dealt with it.

So screw Grafton and his jumped-up self-importance. And screw the bloody walkie-talkie set-up, with its blind spots and its dead areas and all the cheapjack batteries that were forever going on the blink. The house agent's office had at least two telephones, and a quick triple-niner would get a direct line to the Fire Station.

Police Constable Vine could be nasty when the mood so took him. And he could be nasty for no better reason than that, at times, he rather enjoyed a twisted personal satisfaction in being nasty.

It was a misplaced sense of power. It was, as far as Vine was concerned, one chalk-mark in *his* favour, in reply to all those minor annoyances that life had upped and hit him with since he'd joined the force.

He opened the cell door, stared down at the bleary-eyed Timothy Barstow and allowed his lips to curl. Barstow, propped on one elbow on the hard cell bed, blinked back and tried a sick smile for size.

'People like you ... ' Vine's mouth twisted into a scornful smirk. 'People like you shouldn't be allowed to live.'

'It's an opinion,' sighed Barstow.

'You're a disgrace to the human race.'

'I had a skinful last night.'

'You have a skinful every night.'

'Not *every* night,' said Barstow sadly, 'but too often for my own good.'

'Where the hell you get the money from, I don't know.'

'Did I cause much trouble?' asked Barstow.

'Just *being* there,' sneered Vine. 'That's enough.'

'Eh?'

'Just being around causes trouble enough.'

Barstow looked perplexed. He moistened his dry lips with the tip of his tongue, then gave a quick, uncertain smile before he spoke.

'I'm sorry,' he said.

'For being here?'

'I don't think I caused much trouble.'

'Pissed as a newt.'

'Of course. I'm an alcoholic, we both know that.'

'And proud of it.'

'No.'

'That's what you're saying.'

'No. I'm not proud of it.' Barstow was quietly serious. 'Not at all proud of it, Constable. Ashamed, even though the experts insist it's an illness.'

'I think you've fallen in love with little green men,' taunted Vine. 'Or maybe you go in for the cross-eyed pink elephants.'

'Is that what you think?' said Barstow flatly.

'Since you ask.'

'I didn't ask.'

'No?'

'The truth is, I don't really want to know what you think?'

'Don't get too bloody stroppy, Barstow.'

Barstow pushed the single blanket aside and stood up from the bed. He was still a little unsteady on his feet.

He said, 'May I wash, please?'

'Wash?'

'I think I'm allowed to.'

'You're allowed nothing, Barstow.'

'Eh?'

'Nothing!'

'Why?' Barstow's expression reflected his uncertainty. 'What have I done wrong? What have I said?'

'That you're here. That's enough.'

'I cause very little trouble. I never do. I'm not that sort of a drunk. I simply—'

'You're a drunk, Barstow. That's enough. A dirty, stinking, no-good drunk. You're scum. You're—'

'That's as far as you go.' From somewhere deep inside his booze-sodden mind Barstow dragged out the remnants of pride. He said, 'The magistrate will lecture me and then slap a fine around my neck. My wife will throw a holier-than-thou tantrum for the next two days. A lot of people – a lot of good people – have me tagged as a soak, and maybe they're right. But not from *you*, Constable Vine. Not from the one policeman everybody knows is a disgrace to his uniform. Not from . . .'

Reginald Palfrey padded into the bathroom and wished it was any other day but Sunday. Mentally and emotionally he was all wrong for his job. Decent, albeit misguided people would watch him and listen to him on this particular day. On this one day of the week they would certainly listen to him, if only because he was the expert. The 'supposed' expert. The 'accepted' expert. They would listen and mull over his words, perhaps even discuss what he'd said and, always, the fact that the opinions expressed had, on the face of things, been his opinions would give them added weight.

He reached his toothbrush from the rack and squeezed paste across the surface of its bristles. As he began to scour his teeth, his mind took up the ancient chant.

'. . . *The peace of God, which passeth all understanding, keep your hearts and minds in the knowledge and love of God, and of his son Jesus Christ our Lord* . . .'

But there was no peace. Only black and awful doubts. Very frightening doubts. Doubts and guilt. The guilt of suddenly being aware of a personal power and influence you've already misused.

'. . . *and the blessing of God Almighty, the Father, the Son, and the Holy Ghost, be amongst you and remain with you always* . . .'

He swilled out his mouth, then spat the mix of toothpaste and water into the bowl of the hand-basin. As he walked back to the bedroom he found himself wishing he hadn't encouraged Angela to go to Rome with the Women's Institute. And that, too, was wrong. They hadn't had a holiday for more than six years. Neither he nor Angela. And without ever actually pressing the point, he knew her well enough to see the signs. She'd really wanted to see Rome. The Holy City. The seat of that other religion which was, in fact, the cradle of their own.

'I ought not to leave you.'

That's what she'd said. That he ought not to be left alone. That (perhaps) he wasn't strong enough to be allowed, unaccompanied, within the shadows of doubt.

Maybe she'd known. Maybe he'd given some sign of his growing doubts. She was, after all, the daughter of a bishop. She knew all about such things; all about the 'dog-collar' dilemmas; that faith, without what modern man recognised as 'proof', sometimes didn't come easily. That, like water in a leaking bucket, it lessened unless it was continually added to. That the trappings – the vestments, the altar, the chalice and even the church building itself – was not enough.

At that moment Reginald Palfrey should have prayed. Had Angela been with him, he probably would have prayed, and prayer might have helped.

But Angela wasn't there, and he didn't pray. He prepared for the first service of the day without real belief.

From far too few, to far too many. That was the impression of a slightly dazed Police Constable Tidy. From a terribly injured Blythe and himself, all the way to Detective Inspector Fuller, Detective Sergeant Wragg, Police Constable Howes, two ambulance men and three squad cars, each with its own compliment of driver and 'observer'.

Fuller was rapping out instructions.

To the occupants of two of the squad cars: 'You, you, you and you. Take up positions around the bungalow. He's in there. He stays in there until we're ready to let him out.'

To Howes. 'Go with the ambulance. Stay with Sergeant Blythe. When he's had initial treatment, check that he doesn't know something we should know but don't. Then chase the body of Walker at the morgue. Follow things through as link officer in the sudden death sequence.'

To the officers from the third squad car: 'You two, on stand-by. Meanwhile, get on the radio. Pass the good tidings to Headquarters. There's an officer dead. There's an officer badly injured. No need for a circulation. The bastard responsible is still at the scene. Ask that the Assistant Chief be notified. If he thinks the Big Bwana should be disturbed, that's his decision. Ask that Rogate Div. HQ be told to get a shuffle on. We need Crosby out of his pit and at the scene.' Fuller gave a quick, mirthless grin and added, 'Strictly speaking we *don't*. The last thing we need is that nebulous prat arsing things up, but 'proper procedure' insists on certain things, at a time like this.'

To Constable Tidy. 'Do we know who lives here?'

'Arkwright. That's what we're told.'

'And?'

'No milk. No newspapers. Walker was checking the place when he was killed.'

'Unoccupied property?'

'I'd say so. The householder notified us he'd be away.'

'Good.' Fuller nodded. 'Get onto your personal radio. Get whoever's on switchboard duty—'

'Grafton.'

'Good. Get Grafton. Tell him to check the Unoccupied Property Register. Where can this Arkwright be contacted? If he's left a key, who with?'

'Yes, sir.'

Tidy sucked in a deep breath. He seemed relieved to have something to do. He walked towards the front of the bungalow.

Fuller turned to Detective Sergeant Wragg and gave a tight, mirthless smile. He said, 'Our pigeon now, James. Messy, but all ours.'

'Until heavier rank arrives.'

'It won't break the sound barrier.' There was cynicism in the tone. 'This one is tailor-made for mistakes. Big clangers. And it's Sunday.'

'You think?' Wragg looked mildly shocked.

'The rank's just about right,' smiled Fuller. 'Detective Inspector. High enough to carry responsibility and low

61

enough to take the flak.' He moved a shoulder resignedly, then said, 'First question. Do we need shooters?'

'Tidy says he's using an open razor.'

'True. But he knows how to handle it.'

'On a one-to-one basis. Plus, maybe, a surprise element.'

'Meaning?'

'Mob-handed, we could take him.' Wragg made a tiny, hands-open, palm-upwards gesture. 'Give me a free hand – give me a decent kitchen chair – and I'll take him and enjoy doing it.'

'Those days are over,' said Fuller sadly.

'I'll take the bastard on without a kitchen chair,' growled Wragg.

'If the opportunity presents itself, you'll join the queue,' murmured Fuller. Then, 'Time was we could air our muscles a little, but not now.'

'More's the pity.'

'More's the pity.' The echo came from the oldster, who was still standing within listening distance and whom Fuller seemed not to have noticed. He seemed to address his remarks to Wragg as he continued. 'I appreciate how you feel, Officer. One colleague dead and another badly cut up. You want immediate action. You wouldn't be the complete policeman if you didn't.'

'Well, thank *you*!' Wragg's reaction was a mix of startled surprise and polite contempt.

'Ah, yes. Now you, sir.' Fuller turned his attention to the oldster. 'I must ask you to—'

'No.' The oldster shook his head.

'Look, sir. This is—'

'I know what it is, and it's the best thing that's happened since I retired.'

'Retired?'

'Forgive me.' There was slightly exaggerated

politeness in the oldster's voice. 'Might I ask, what rank do you carry?'

'Rank?'

'I take it you're the senior officer at the scene.'

'For the moment,' agreed Fuller.

'And your rank?'

'Inspector. Detective Inspector.'

'Good.' The oldster enjoyed a quick, tight smile. 'I outrank you. Chief Superintendent. Gowan. Chief Superintendent Gowan of the Hong Kong Police.'

'*Late* of the Hong Kong Police,' corrected Fuller. 'You've already said that you're retired.'

'Ah!'

'And even if you weren't retired, Rogate-on-Sands isn't yet part of the Hong Kong City beat.'

Gowan scowled momentary annoyance then said, 'I won't insult your intelligence by mentioning the fact that I "know" certain people.'

'Well, thank you, sir.'

'But I *do*,' added Gowan petulantly.

'Good.' It was a dead, expressionless response. A non-word with which to block any attempt at intimidation.

Gowan suddenly looked distinctly unhappy. Almost pleadingly he said, 'I won't get in the way.'

'Look, sir.' Fuller blew out his cheeks a little. 'This thing might end up a very nasty—'

'Inspector, forgive me, but have you ever crossed swords with the triads?'

'Rogate-on-Sands,' sighed Fuller. 'I can't say we often—'

'I should have said hatchets. Hatchets, not swords. Hatchets are their chosen weapons, Inspector. Sharpened. Sharpened to an edge on a par with the cut-throat used on your Sergeant. They're quite horrific weapons, Inspector. The injuries they can inflict have to be seen

63

to be believed.'

'Look, sir.' Fuller gave a sad shake of the head. 'I can't give you permission to get mixed up in this lot. You know that. *You*, of all people, know. Whoever you are, whatever you were, I just can't—'

'Just let me stay,' pleaded Gowan. 'That's all. To get the "feel" of the incident, not to *do* anything. Not unless you want me to, of course. But, y'know, just to be part of law-enforcement again. On the fringe. No more, but just that. Please!'

Fuller hesitated, then with obvious reluctance said, 'You keep well out of the way.'

'Of course.'

'You just watch. Nothing more.'

'That's clearly understood, Inspector.'

'You don't get under anybody's feet. You keep well clear of any possible firing line. And, when the weight arrives, those who give *me* orders, you blow.'

## 0745 Hours

Crosby had made up his mind. No messing. No fancy excuses. He was going to find the man responsible for C Beat if it took him all day. He was going to find him, and then he was going to fizz him. Which, in turn, would be something of a novelty for Crosby. Because of his nature – he was something of a coward and therefore wasn't too keen on manufacturing enemies – Crosby hadn't used many Form 252s in the course of his service. But by God, he was going to use one this time. He was going to enjoy using one. Misconduct Forms were *made* for this sort of situation. To take the steam out of coppers who figured themselves smarter than the system, fly enough to get away with just about anything, and dump them firmly back on their smart-arsed rumps, which was where they belonged.

What Crosby didn't know was that Police Constable Wood knew all about the presence of the Rogate-on-Sands Superintendent on C Beat.

In a back-to-front, left-handed-thread way Wood was quite a copper. He knew every vantage point on C Beat. He knew where he could see and not be seen; every cul-de-sac and back alley; every short cut and hiding-place. He knew exactly where Crosby's car was and which part of the beat it was making for. Indeed he'd already been almost within touching distance of the car as it passed a row of shops.

And Wood was cunning. He knew Crosby and had already weighed up the opposition.

It was a calculated risk, if only because the Superintendent was known as a man given to consternation and alarm. The trick, therefore, was to keep out of sight until the initial annoyance had burned itself out; until anger had given way to worry. Things happen to coppers. They are no longer the well-beloved Dixon-of-Dock-Green-PC-Plod figures of the fairly recent past. They can be cornered. They can be ambushed. Terrible things happen to them.

And, sometimes – often – what happens to a beat constable is taken as a reflection upon the manner in which a divisional officer runs his area of control. A divisional officer like Crosby, for example. A sloppy, slap-happy divisional officer, given to ducking from under. A divisional officer who, if the spectre of something he can't dodge gets up and haunts him, is capable of worrying himself into a state of dithering panic.

That was what Wood wanted.

He wanted Crosby to start sweating.

The number of policemen at the scene was mounting. A

65

fourth squad car had arrived. Grafton had been busy spreading the news and seeking reinforcements from neighbouring sections.

Fuller said, 'Next of kin.'

Wragg said, 'Ah!' in sympathy.

'Walker and Blythe. They're both married.'

'Quite.'

'Their wives have to be notified.'

Wragg said, 'Blythe's wife goes out to work.' He made it sound like something of which Mrs Blythe should be ashamed.

'Where?' asked Fuller.

'One of the hotels, I think. Relief receptionist.'

Fuller checked the time with his wrist watch.

He said, 'Relief. That could mean Sunday. If so, she might not have left home yet. If we get on the blower...' From beyond Wragg's shoulder he saw Gowan frown and gently shake his head. Fuller continued, 'But that would be a bad way of doing it.'

Wragg looked momentarily perplexed.

'Telephoning,' explained Fuller. 'Asking her not to go to work today. Not until we've seen her.'

'Oh.'

'It would make her worry.'

'Of course.'

'She'd be in no condition to receive bad news. Better to go directly to where she works. Then, if she is there, have one of her workmates hold her hand.'

Wragg nodded grudging agreement.

Fuller said, 'We need a policewoman.'

'Grant,' suggested Wragg.

'You think?'

'A motherly type.'

'I'd say matronly type, but she'll do.' Fuller turned to one of the spare constables and asked, 'Have you your car with you?'

66

'Yes, sir.'

'A lousy job for you, old son.'

'Oh!'

'But somebody has to be lumbered with it. Call in at Rogate DHQ. Get the home address of Sergeant Blythe, and the home address of Constable Walker. Find where Woman Police Sergeant Grant lives, then go and pick her up. Got that so far?'

'Yes, sir.'

'Fine. From there, to the Memorial Hospital. You'll find Constable Howes there, with Sergeant Blythe. Get to know the state of play. We know Walker's dead. We want to know how badly Blythe has been cut. Then, when you both know exactly what you're talking about, break the news. First to Mrs Walker. Then to Mrs Blythe.'

'Yes, sir.' The constable sounded distinctly unhappy.

'Not you personally. Sergeant Grant. She should know them both. You're there to pick anybody up who flakes out.'

'Yes, sir.' The constable still sounded unhappy.

Fuller ended, 'Mrs Blythe might be out at work. If she is – if Sergeant Grant decides she should stay with Mrs Walker – contact her at work, and get one of the women who work with her to lend a hand at breaking the news.'

'Yes, sir.'

'Then get back here and let us know how things have worked out.'

Fuller felt a little foolish, but he couldn't help himself. He glanced towards Gowan and felt a silly glow of pleasure as he saw the approving smile on the ex-Hong Kong policeman's lips.

Bob Grafton walked from the tiny, alcove-like room that housed the telephone switchboard and the microphone which linked DHQ with the patrol men's personal radios.

Grafton's upper lip showed the faintest sheen of sweat.

He'd been taking a few risks, if only because he was almost flying blind as far as Audsley Avenue was concerned. As always, until a direct radio and telephone link was established, the unfortunate goon yelling for assistance might be asking for too much or, indeed, asking for too little.

There'd been a murder and there'd been a maiming, he *thought*.

The creep responsible for both the murder and the maiming was still at the scene, he *thought*.

But where the hell was Wood? And why the hell couldn't Fairclough go to Audsley Avenue and make himself useful?

Meanwhile good old, live-dangerously Grafton had spread the word, and Fuller and Wragg would soon have enough common-or-garden coppers to keep them happy, he hoped.

Vine was in the outer office. He was leaning against the public counter and (or so Grafton thought) he was looking distinctly off-colour. Pale, almost to the point of green.

'Something the matter?' asked Grafton.

'Eh?' Vine blinked, then looked startled.

'Something the matter?' repeated Grafton.

'No. Why do you ask. Why should—'

'You look ill.'

'Ill?'

'Off-colour. As if you're—'

'I'm not ill. Why should I be ill?'

'I'm sorry. I didn't mean to suggest anything offensive. Just that you look, y'know, not well.'

'I'm fine.'

'Good.'

'Fine.'

Grafton switched topics of conversation in an attempt to steady a rocking boat.

68

He said, 'How's Barstow?'

'Barstow?' The impression was that Vine shied away from the name, much as a horse shies away from a fence it thinks is too high to jump. Vine gave a tiny, throat-clearing cough, then said, 'Barstow's all right. Why worry about Barstow?'

'Has he had his breakfast?'

'Barstow?'

'Yeah. I thought you'd been—'

'What's all the sudden hassle about Barstow?'

'Nothing. Just that—'

'Suddenly, Barstow's bloody important.'

'I'm not saying that. I was just asking—'

'Sod Barstow. Eh? He can have his bloody breakfast when *I* decide.'

The day had cleared its throat, rubbed its eyes and was beginning to gather its wits together. Even on D Beat which, by any ordinary yardstick, wasn't really a 'holiday-town' quarter but more of a snooty, neat and select residential area of a town that happened to be on the coast, things were starting to move.

The bread-winners – the office-workers, the local authority officials, the commuters, the white- and blue-collar workers, the school-teachers, the doctors, the accountants, the solicitors, the whole world of non-productive wage-earners – were leaving their beds, sniffing the morning air, strolling in the handkerchief-sized gardens, opening their garage doors, prior to moving the car to the drive for its weekly clean and polish and generally showing signs of increased activity.

The 'senior citizens' too, the elderly ladies and gentlemen, even they, who had no real reason for leaving their beds until they felt so inclined, were up and about.

The day had truly begun.

An increase in pedestrian and vehicular traffic meant that the eyes of the town were gradually being directed towards Audsley Avenue. Something was decidedly 'up'. All this activity. All these coppers. Something had, undoubtedly, happened.

The elderly man at Number Seventy-Four conquered his normal reticence and wandered down the street to speak with Constable Tidy.

'Is something wrong?'

'Yes, sir, you could say that.'

Tidy watched a duo of motor patrol officers spacing 'No Parking' cones along the pavement edge.

'At Bob's place?' pressed the elderly man.

'Here, at Twenty-Six.'

'Aye. Bob's place.'

'I understand Mr Arkwright's away.' Tidy tried for a further verification of what was already known.

'Oh, aye. A shooting-and-fishing holiday. That's what he told me.'

'Shooting? Fishing?'

'Out in the Yorkshire Dales somewhere. He has a friend from his schooldays who owns a farm at Nidderdale. That's where he is.'

'Nice weather for it,' observed Tidy.

'Aye. I saw him off last Saturday. For two weeks.' The elderly man smiled gently and shook his head. 'A great one for shooting, Bob. I don't think he's too keen on fishing, but he took two of his guns with him.'

'Guns?'

Tidy felt an uncomfortable tingling between his shoulder blades, like ants scurrying up and down his spine.

'He collects them,' amplified the elderly man. 'Mostly antiques. Mostly shotguns.'

'Mostly?'

'He has a few more up-to-date models, of course.'

70

'How many?'

'What?'

'Guns? Shotguns? Any sort of guns? Guns capable of being used?'

'Oh, I don't know. Not for sure.'

'Guess?'

'I've seen four. At least four. Twelve-bore. Double-barrel and single-barrel. And a couple of muzzle-loaders. He goes in for guns. He's very knowledgeable. He collects them. Gives lectures to gun clubs occasionally.'

'Will there . . . ' Tidy tried to keep the concern from his voice. 'Are there likely to be guns in the house now? At this moment?'

'Oh, aye. For sure.'

'How many?'

'It's hard to say.'

'More than one?'

'Oh, aye. I should ask Mrs Littlewood. She might know.'

'Mrs Littlewood?'

'The cleaning lady. She does for him twice a week. Tuesdays and Thursdays. When he's on holiday, she calls in to check things are all right. She's in there now. If you ask her . . . '

'*Now!*'

'Eh?'

'You say she's in there now?'

'She comes early,' explained the elderly man. 'She was here at just after six. I know that. I noticed. She cleans for us every Wednesday and . . . '

The elderly man closed his mouth. Tidy was no longer within listening distance. He'd turned and was hurrying towards Detective Sergeant Wragg.

*

71

'An arson job,' assessed the fire chief. 'At the very least an attempted arson.'

'Yeah.'

Fairclough nodded and watched the fireman playing a jet onto the burned rags.

'Charring, behind the door,' explained the fire chief. 'Just under the letter-box. Common enough, but nasty. Causes damage. That, and a lot of inconvenience.'

Fairclough said, 'Yeah,' again and wondered if the Fire Service ever realised that they, too, caused damage. Sometimes unnecessary damage. And inconvenience.

They used too much water. They squirted with wild and careless abandon. The floor of the house agent's office was already swimming in almost an inch of water. Dirty water, with bits of charred cloth floating around on its surface.

Out in the arcade the rubber-neckers were already gathering. Counter staff and shopkeepers who worked in the arcade and who had come in for a quick, Sunday-morning dust down and stock-take. And even at this hour, men and women who used the arcade as a short-cut. The crowd was building up and, as Fairclough knew from past experience, they'd soon make a gathering big enough to attract attention and that, in turn, would pull in even more gawpers.

He said, 'I need a hand. I'll be back. I'll just go and radio for help to keep the odds and sods from under our feet.'

The 'odds and sods' were also collecting in Audsley Avenue. The area had been taped off. Cones had been positioned alongside the kerb. Police cars were parked; some still had their blue lights revolving on the roof.

A clapped-out Ford braked to a halt, its bonnet almost touching the 'Crime Area – Keep Out' tapes, and the driver wound down the window to speak to a uniformed constable who'd strolled up. The driver left the engine of the car running.

In the garden at the rear of Number Twenty-Six, Fuller, Wragg and Tidy were having a very serious conversation. They talked in low voices, and their words carried a lot of worry.

'That's all we need,' muttered Wragg. 'A homicidal bastard in a house full of guns.'

'He obviously hasn't found them yet.' Tidy tried to be optimistic.

'He will.'

'We need the Tactical Firearms Group,' said Fuller. It was obviously a decision he didn't enjoy making. 'We also need to get people out of nearby houses, in case it comes to a straightforward shoot-out.'

'Happy days!' growled Wragg.

Tidy asked, 'What about the woman? Mrs Littlewood?'

'Right.' Fuller took a deep breath, squared his shoulders and spoke directly to Wragg. 'Get to a squad car, James. Then get on the air. We need the TFG boys here as soon as possible. Let the Chief Constable's office know what's happening. If we *have* to start a shooting war, we need the top man here to make the fancy decisions.' He paused, then continued, 'Next, get to know the address of this Littlewood woman. Tell DHQ to send somebody round. I want to know whether she's still at home and, if not, where she might be. I want her found, or I want to *know* she's inside this bungalow.'

As Wragg turned to leave Fuller added, 'Oh, yes. Get onto the Telecom people. I want a link-up with the phone inside the bungalow. This character, whoever he is, we need to be able to talk to him.'

Wragg passed a happy-looking Gowan as he made his way to the gate and the nearest squad car.

## 0800 Hours

Beth Daniels was worried. She wasn't yet afraid, but the truth was she'd never seen her husband like this before. She'd seen him lose his temper maybe half-a-dozen times since they'd married, and each time she'd felt a slight twinge of worry. Daniels was a quiet, moderate man, but on those occasions he'd hinted at a capacity for frightening fury. And now it was here again. But this time, not raging annoyance; not blazing, high-octane anger. Instead something much worse.

Daniels' present temper was a cold, bleak emotion. It was glacial and seemed quite indifferent to any external influence. Beth had tried tears; by screwing up her face and indulging in a great bore of self-pity, she'd managed a few trickles down her cheeks. But Daniels' tight smile had had no more warmth than permafrost.

She took a deep breath, then began, 'You—'

She gave a sobbing, choking sound, and Daniels waited.

'Y'know. You won't—'

'What?' The question was quietly spoken, but without a hint of feeling.

'I mean . . .' Suddenly she was tongue-tied.

'I know what?'

'I wouldn't hurt you, Charlie. Not *hurt* you.'

'What a stupid thing to say.'

'You know I wouldn't hurt you. You must know that.'

'No. I don't know any such thing.'

'If – if you think—'

'I think you talk too much.'

'Oh.'

'Save it for somebody willing to listen. Save it for Chris. He might be interested in what you have to say.'

'But not you?' she pleaded.

74

'I've been stone deaf for too long. Far too long. Shout it, sing it, scream it – it doesn't make much difference. I don't hear any more.'

As Wragg ducked into a parked squad car in order to radio a string of instructions to Force Headquarters and Rogate-on-Sands DHQ the uniformed constable raised the tape and allowed the battered Ford to roll gently into the restricted area. It parked at the kerb, near the bungalow, and Tom Tolby climbed from the driving seat.

Tolby wore an open-necked, lumberjack-style shirt, twill trousers and sneakers. He was clean-shaven and wore his hair in an old-fashioned, short-back-and-sides cut. He looked what he was: a decent, middle-aged man with a contented wife, a crippling mortgage, three happy children and a badly paid job on a provincial newspaper. But he was a happy man; he liked the work, liked Rogate-on-Sands and loved his family. Despite the fact that he never quite cleared off all his debts, his happiness showed and (in spite of his job) the policemen of the town liked him. He knew when to ask a question and, more importantly, when to keep quiet; he knew when to push his luck, but he also knew when to let things settle; he knew when to print things and when to do a strictly-off-the-record routine.

Tolby passed a worried-looking Howes and a puzzled Gowan as he opened the gate and walked up the path, but Fuller nodded a friendly enough greeting.

Tolby said, 'I was given the tip-off.'

'It would be a waste of breath to ask the name of your snout, of course?'

'A waste of breath,' agreed Tolby. Then, after this routine exchange, he added, 'It's obviously serious.'

'Uh-huh.'

'What's happened?'

'One police officer murdered. One police officer badly injured.'

Tolby pursed his lips into a silent whistle.

In a sad voice Fuller continued, 'We're getting the shooters out. The maniac responsible is holed up inside.'

'Do we know who?'

Fuller shook his head and growled, 'Coloured. Beyond that, nothing.'

'Just that he's in there.' Tolby paused, then added, 'I've passed the griff onto the local radio.'

'You have a job to do,' sighed Fuller.

'That's all. No details. Just that something's happened. You can give them what details you feel like releasing when they get here.'

'And you?'

'From here on, I print only what you want me to print.'

'Photographs?'

'Colin should be here within the next fifteen minutes or so. He'll keep his camera in its case until I give him the go-ahead.'

Fuller's lips moved into a quick smile and said, 'You'll never make Fleet Street, Tolby.'

'You're out of date, Inspector. Fleet Street is a ghost town these days. They've crossed the river. And they're more interested in nudes than news. The only honest-to-God reporting is done out in the sticks.'

At about the time Tolby was making naughty remarks about nationally renowned by-liners, Superintendent Andrew Lewis Crosby was experiencing some of the less happy moments of his life.

It could be said that Crosby brought it on himself; that, if he'd behaved in a more rational manner; if his sheer pig-headedness hadn't forced him to lose all sense of proportion; if he'd accepted that some, if not all, street men take the first couple of hours of an Early Shift as smoothly as possible; if, in other words, he hadn't been so determined to concentrate all his attention on knocking the C Beat man from his perch; all these 'ifs' and it might not have happened.

But it *did* happen, and it was not at all enjoyable.

Crosby had become suspicious. Gradually a possibility had been born, grown and nurtured in his mind. What if Constable Wood was deliberately playing catch-me-if-you-can? What if this cunning pavement-basher was intentionally keeping out of sight?

As the possibility dawned, Crosby began to systematically quarter the streets and roads of C Beat. As he passed the mouths of linking streets he craned his neck and peered to make sure no uniformed figure was nipping out of sight.

Had he kept up the search he might well have caught up with the crafty Police Constable Wood. Indeed, had it been possible for Crosby to look in two directions at once, things might have ended very differently.

Unfortunately it wasn't Crosby's lucky day.

Each time he leaned forward over the steering wheel to check the streets on his left, there was a tendency for the car to drift to the near-side. Then, after correction, the car was a little closer to its near-side kerb than it had been previously. Given a long enough road, with sufficient offshoots to its left, what happened was bound to happen.

It did.

Crosby felt the front wheels of the car mount the pavement. He jerked his head and for a hair's-breadth of a second saw the concrete lamp standard, then the bonnet smashed into the reinforced concrete at about twenty-five miles an hour. Crosby was thrown forward and his seat belt grabbed him across the chest and waist, but not before he'd cracked his forehead against the edge of the pulled-down sun visor and knocked himself cold.

He wasn't out long.

When he returned to the land of the living he could have been forgiven for wishing his state of unconsciousness had lasted a little longer. The woman had the statistics of a cheese straw and the hawking, grating voice any self-respecting crow would have hurriedly disowned, and she was letting rip.

'You stupid man. You stupid, *stupid* man.' She fairly spat the words out. 'No wonder people get killed on the road. With drivers like you around, no *wonder*. We aren't even safe on the pavement. Have you been drinking? Is that it? *Can* you drive? Very obviously, you *can't*. All the road – the full width of the road – and it's only by the grace of God you didn't run me down. I'm not even on the road. I'm not even *near* the road. But you still—'

Fuller said, 'I want the street cleared. I want everybody with a view of this bungalow out of their homes before the TFG arrive. I want them well clear of any firing line.'

'Don't you think that's over-reacting a bit, boss?' murmured Wragg.

'No.'

'I think you're wrong.'

'Do you?'

'We're not even sure he has a gun. Until now it's only been an open razor.'

'Sergeant.' Fuller's tone held tight exasperation. 'I'm giving instructions. An order, if you like. What I am not doing is tossing out a suggestion for open discussion.'

'Look, I only—'

'Do it, Sergeant. Get everybody moved out. And if

78

they refuse to move, note their names and addresses and the fact that they've been strongly advised to get clear of any action.'

'Yes, sir.' The words were stiff and formal.

'And, Sergeant?'

'Yes, sir.'

'You should realise there's a possibility, even a probability, that guns *are* in this bungalow. I can either risk His Nibs finding one of those bloody guns and banging away in all directions, or I can suffer your childish sulks. So there's no real choice, is there?'

Police Constable 221 Henry Vine had allowed his natural ill-temper to land him in trouble. But like others of his kind he didn't see it that way. The way *he* saw it, he'd been provoked beyond the point of all reasonable endurance.

Nobody was going to believe him, of course. The finks who decided these things would take the word of a drunk against the word of a copper.

Nevertheless . . .

Barstow had asked for it. Asked for it? He'd sat up and begged for it. He (Vine) was a fully authorised law-enforcement officer. He wasn't some jumped-up, penny-a-dozen, ragged-arsed nobody. He was a man to be respected. He had the power to arrest and detain. He had the authority to hold up his hand and stop motor vehicles, regardless of who was behind the steering wheel. He represented the law. The Criminal Law.

He wasn't here to take slaver by the bucketful from a no-good soak who'd been banged up for the night in a police cell.

Which was great, except . . .

The majority of mugs had different ideas. Strange ideas. Stupid ideas. Blythe, for example. Even a prize prat like Crosby. They had a fancy name for it – Police

79

Public Relations – but it was a crappy name for a crappy idea. Buttering up to everybody, including the scum of the streets. Busting a gut for the sake of cheap publicity, that's what it boiled down to.

Well, if that's what Blythe and his kind wanted, let them get on with it. Let them roll into hell on their own custom-built roller-skates, but don't be surprised when the louts rule the streets and the hooligans rule the terraces. Anyway, that way of policing wasn't for Constable Vine. Not bloody likely! Make the bastards crawl a little. Put the fear of Christ into them. That was the way. The old-fashioned way. The only way. And it worked!

Which was nothing less than the truth, but . . .

Barstow might turn nasty. Not much doubt that he would. And too many mamby-pamby people would take *his* side against any reasonable argument offered by a police officer who happened to be proud of the uniform he'd worn for years.


## 0815 Hours

Crosby blinked his way back to full consciousness slowly, and with a great urge to puke. He tried to tune out the raspings of the woman but couldn't. He heard her well before he'd worked out why he couldn't move without hindrance, what it was that held him tight against the driving seat and why the car had come to a sudden stop.

'. . . but you still nearly ran me down. Here, on the pavement. Minding my own business. Walking home from church. Nowhere *near* the road, but you still . . .'

'It's all right, missus. I'll take over.'

Had he been asked, only a few seconds earlier, Crosby would have sworn he'd never again be grateful for the sound of Constable Wood's voice. Indeed, until the car had hit the lamp standard Crosby had actively hated Wood; he'd been anxious to fizz him; he'd been working out ways and means of fixing that common-or-garden copper tighter than the skin on the average side-drum. He'd been looking forward to 'doing' Wood, but *good*!

Now Crosby breathed, 'Thank God,' and relaxed back into a state of half-consciousness.

As if from beneath a few thicknesses of blanket, Crosby heard the woman squawking her name and address, then giving a highly sententious description of the shunt-up. Her version, of course. Not the true version. Not Crosby's version.

She left the scene. There was a pause.

Then Wood's voice said, 'Now, sir. We'd better get you off to hospital.'

'Eh?' Crosby fought to force some degree of understanding into his brain.

'Hospital, sir.'

'Constable Wood, where the devil have you been?'

'I'm here, sir.'

'Of course, but where have you *been*?'

'As soon as I heard, sir. I didn't know it was you.'

'That's not what I—'

'Just that somebody had driven his car into a lamp standard.'

'I didn't—'

'Sir?'

'I wasn't—'

'Wasn't what, sir?'

'It wasn't at all like that. Dammit, I was—'

'I'm sorry, sir, but if you're about to give me a verbal account of what happened, I think I'd better caution you before you continue.'

'*Wha-at!*'

'I might have to repeat it in court, sir.'

81

'In *where*?'

Behind Wood's shoulder, Crosby could see a small crowd already gathering.

The man with the clipped moustache, wearing a panama and a regimental tie snapped, 'What's happened here?'

The stout man, wearing half-moon specs and carrying a library book under one arm, said, 'Some clown out all night, at a guess.'

'Ah!'

'Stewed as a prune.'

'Good God!'

'Can't even keep the car on the road.'

'What is he? Navy?'

'Corps of Commissionaires, at a guess.'

'Ah!'

'You see, sir,' emphasised Wood. Then, 'We'd better get you to hospital for a check up.'

'I will,' breathed Crosby.

'What's that, sir?'

'I'll get you for this, Wood. As sure as God made green apples, and if it takes forever.'

'Should I make a note of that, sir?' asked Wood innocently. 'For the court appearance?'

She was a roly-poly woman. She'd been a roly-poly teenager and, before that, a roly-poly child. She'd grown used to it but she'd never grown to *like* it. Like most heavily built people she was a slim woman trapped for life inside a fat woman's body.

She had trouble finding clothes which didn't make her look even plumper than she was. The fashion experts insisted upon advising 'vertical stripes' as a means of disguising what they stupidly described as 'the fuller figer'. But who were *they* kidding? She wished to hell that's all she was lumbered with, a 'fuller figer'. She

82

was fat, my friend. And fat is something nobody can hide away behind vertical stripes. They don't stay vertical, they *bend*.

Thus, and as a mask behind which she might hide, she was blunt and almost cruelly honest. Especially with herself and about herself. She'd heard every gag about her shape and her weight. She'd even invented a few herself.

But all that was a gag. Deep down, she hurt. Deep down, she was a dishy female, buried inside an obese body from which she'd never get out. Inside her secret self, she wept. Inside the hard shell of mild obscenities and mock heartlessness, she was never far from tears.

She was a policewoman. More than that, she was a *good* policewoman; a uniformed sergeant. And she sat alongside the uniformed constable as they drove towards the home address of Police Constable 899 John Walker, towards what had once been his home address.

Fuller had picked the Constable at random. He'd been wearing the nearest uniform to Fuller, when Fuller had remembered that next-of-kin had to be notified. Therefore Fuller had pounced.

That was how things went. At a murder enquiry everything came first. Everything had Number One priority. Checking that the victim was dead. Not touching the victim. Yelling for a medic to certify death. Screaming for the various specialist services. Making sure that nothing was removed from the scene. Checking that nobody left the scene. Stopping people who weren't at the scene when the crime was committed from wandering onto the scene. Keeping your hands in your pockets. Keeping your mouth shut. Making sure everybody else kept their hands in their pockets and their mouths shut. And – but of course – notifying the next-of-kin.

All these things had to be done first. They all took

priority over everything else. They were all of paramount importance.

So said 'the book', but the guy who'd written the book had never officiated at a real-life murder enquiry.

That's how he knew all these things.

Fuller had remembered some of the priorities and, when he'd remembered the next-of-kin bit, he'd roped in an unknown copper called Yates. Police Constable 1313 Walter Yates.

Yates said, 'You'd better show me the way, Sergeant. I don't know Rogate-on-Sands too well.'

'First right, then second left. You'll see the Hospital sign on your right,' said WPS Grant. She added, 'Where are you from, lover boy?'

'Eh?' Yates blinked, then said, 'Acton Division. I was, y'know, roped in to help.'

'You've pulled the short straw. One of the lousy jobs,' she observed.

'Somebody has to.' He allowed a smile to touch his lips, and said, 'It includes you.'

'Me?' She chuckled and the car seemed to shudder slightly as it took the strain. 'It has its advantages. It's better than stripping off and lying on top of the bed, trying to keep cool in this weather.'

'Jesus!' The mental vision made Yates swallow.

'Wet and sweaty,' she cooed. 'Not fit for much more than lying on your back and letting *anything* happen.'

'The Telecom people', as Fuller had called them, had come up trumps. The telephone engineer had arrived within minutes. He'd shinned up a nearby pole and linked telephone wires to telephone wires. Returning to the pavement he'd reeled out more wire, then linked in a handset by the side of the bungalow.

'It's all yours,' he'd said, and waved a hand to show that the job had been completed.

'Thanks.'

Fuller had brought two collapsible chairs from a garden hut. He'd lifted the hand-set onto one and settled himself on the other.

'Just dial the number?' he'd asked.

'No need. Just lift the receiver and turn the handle.'

'Thanks,' repeated Fuller. Then, 'I have to ask you to move well out of sight of this place now. Things could turn a little hairy.'

The engineer raised quizzical eyebrows.

'If things go wrong,' amplified Fuller. 'If we make any real mistakes.'

The engineer nodded his understanding, said, 'Good luck,' and walked back to his waiting van.

## 0830 Hours

Fairclough almost staggered into Rogate-on-Sands Police Station. He looked grubby. He felt grubby. His temper was such that he was ready for a good, old-fashioned, drag-'em-out-then-kick-'em-in-the-teeth-for-luck argument with anybody.

Grafton's eyes widened and he began, 'What the hell—'

'Don't *you* start,' warned Fairclough.

'Eh?'

'Just be warned.'

'Hey, look. I—'

'That prize prick of a manager.'

'Which manager?'

'The bloody house agents.'

'Oh!'

'Sounding off about the mess.'

'Which house agents?'

'The bloody place could have been burned down.'

85

'You know there's been a murder?' Grafton made it part-question and part-accusation.

'What the hell would you have liked me to do?' Fairclough glared. 'Let the bloody place burn to the ground?'

'Harry.' Grafton tried soothing tactics. 'People round here are going bananas, believe me. Johnny Walker's copped it. Blythe's been knifed badly. Somewhere in Audsley Avenue. All hell's popping. I've had to call in men from neighbouring divisions. You have no idea.'

'I heard.' Fairclough did nothing to hide his peevishness. 'I couldn't help but hear. You were bawling and shouting all over the walkie-talkie air-waves. But Christ Almighty, I had a shop fire on my hands. I couldn't leave that to burn.'

'And Vic Wood. And Crosby.' The conversation seemed to be developing into a form of competition. '*And* you. People won't see the truth, that a microphone isn't much good if people aren't going to answer.'

'There are blind spots. Dead areas.'

Grafton's expression showed absolute disbelief.

'Hell's teeth!' exploded Fairclough. 'Even you should know that. A shopping arcade, for God's sake. Walkie-talkies don't work in those sort of places. An old-fashioned whistle would do more good.'

'I know.' Grafton saw no reason why he, too, couldn't display a degree of peevishness. 'Some of you buggers seem to *live* in dead areas. Think I don't know the gag? Find a nice, handy dead area and you have a ready-made cop-out. That's where you are, where you *claim* to be when you don't feel like answering. That's where you are when you want to offload unwanted crap onto some other poor sod's shoulders. You think I was born yesterday?'

'Oh, bollocks.'

It was not a very erudite remark. It was not meant to

86

be. Nor was it, in any way, an argument clincher. It was, if anything, a rather vulgar, verbal full-stop; the end of a sentence, the end of a paragraph, the slightly foul-mouthed end of a very pointless argument.

Fairclough uttered it then stalked out of the room, along the passage and into the Gents' Toilet. He was grubby, he was soot-speckled and his clothes and shoes were in need of a quick brushing and polishing.

As he pushed open the swing doors of the toilets, he saw the spots of blood on the tiled floor. They were 5p-sized splashes and they led to the corner, around which were a row of wash-basins. Indeed, the wash-basins were Fairclough's destination.

As he rounded the corner, he saw Barstow.

Timothy Barstow was bent low over one of the basins. The water in the basin was coloured a deep pink from the blood he was washing from his face.

'Hey! What the hell?' exclaimed Fairclough.

'Eh?'

Barstow hadn't heard the Constable enter the toilets. He lifted a dripping face and exposed split lips and bleeding gums.

Fairclough said, 'What goes on?'

'I tripped and fell.' Barstow tried hard to smile, but the movement of his facial muscles brought the blood spilling from his mouth and dripping from the end of his chin.

'You *tripped*? You *fell*?' The double question was heavy with disbelief.

'Uh-huh.' Barstow returned to the business of splashing water onto the area around his mouth. His words had a bubbling quality. 'I tripped against the cell bed.'

'Just like that?'

'Uh-huh.'

'Was Vine there?'

87

Fairclough slipped off his tunic and hung it on a nearby wall hook.

'Mr Fairclough.' Barstow continued to scoop water and dash it onto his battered face. 'Accept it, eh? Nobody was there.'

'You were in the cell?'

'Yes, sir.'

'Tell me, how did you get out of the cell?' Fairclough took a brush from a nearby locker and began to brush his trousers. 'The cell door was locked.'

'No, sir.'

'It wasn't locked?'

'No, sir. It wasn't locked.'

'Why?'

'I think Mr Vine must have left it unlocked.'

'Vine?'

'I think he must have forgotten to lock it when he left.'

Fairclough finished brushing his trousers and started to brush his hung-up tunic. He finished brushing and returned the brush to its locker before he spoke again.

He said, 'Why are you lying, Barstow?'

'I'm not lying, Mr Fairclough.'

'Are you so frightened of an arsehole like Vine?'

'Why should I lie, Mr Fairclough?'

'You tell me.'

'No, sir, I'm not lying.'

'Does Grafton know about this?'

'What's that, Mr Fairclough?'

'About Vine thumping you?'

'I didn't say—'

'You didn't have to say.'

'Oh.'

'I know Vine.'

Fairclough ran hot water into the basin next to Barstow's. He soaped his hands and glanced sideways to where the miserable man was still splashing water onto his face.

Barstow muttered. 'I don't want trouble, Mr Fairclough.'

'Trouble?'

'You know what I mean.'

'No.'

'I don't want trouble, that's all. I end up in the cells too often.'

'Being knocked around?'

'No, sir. That's not what I'm—'

'Being thumped *isn't* trouble?'

'I'm not an aggressive man, Mr Fairclough.'

'No.'

'Not usually.'

'You're a drunk,' said Fairclough, gently and without criticism. He added, 'You're not alone.'

'I'm weak,' mumbled Barstow. 'Stupid.'

'That, too, perhaps.'

'I know these things.' Barstow moved from the basin and pulled a paper towel from its holder. He dabbed his face as he continued. 'I know exactly what I am. I don't kid myself.'

'Good.'

'But I'm no trouble-maker.'

'A bit of a nuisance sometimes.' Fairclough pulled a paper towel from the holder. He smiled and added, 'That's only an opinion, of course.'

Barstow said, 'But this time I asked for it.'

'Is that a fact?'

'I shouldn't have said what I said.'

'Not to Vine?' teased Fairclough.

'I think I asked for what I got, sir. I've nothing to complain about. Mr Vine's only human.'

'Is he?' said Fairclough grimly. 'It's nice to know. I hadn't noticed.

*

The Assistant Chief Constable was very young for the rank. More than that, he looked even younger than he was. He had a peaches-and-cream complexion and his hair and eyebrows were corn-coloured, with just the barest hint of sand. He was strictly a career copper, and the nearest thing to a yuppie the service was ever likely to tolerate.

He knew the book from cover to cover; he could recite it, word for word, forwards or backwards. In his quest for quick promotion he'd jumped from force to force, like a flea on a griddle; forever scanning the pages of *Police Review* in the hope of bettering himself.

Last night he'd been out late with the local Freemasonry crowd. He'd boasted a little and drank a lot. He'd bought himself something of a hangover and, as always, it hadn't been cheap.

He drawled phoney incomprehension as he talked to Police Constable Grafton over the telephone.

'Doesn't your Detective know?' he demanded.

'Detective Inspector, sir.' Grafton wasn't too keen on the ACC. Moreover, parochial loyalty seemed to demand that the proper rank be acknowledged.

'I beg your pardon?'

'Detective *Inspector*, sir. Inspector Fuller.'

'What's your name, Constable?'

'Grafton, sir. Number nine-eight-nine Grafton.'

'Tread a little more carefully, Constable Grafton.'

'Sir?'

'Don't contradict Assistant Chief Constables *too* many times.'

'No, sir.'

'And remind your friend, *Inspector* Fuller, that only divisional officers – which means Superintendents and above – have the authority to call out the Tactical

90

Firearms Group. Your Superintendent Crosby, for example, has the authority. *Not* your Detective Inspector Fuller.'

Grafton didn't answer.

The ACC said, 'Do you hear me, Grafton?'

'Yes, sir.'

'Be wise, Constable.'

'Yes, sir.'

Grafton muttered, 'You stupid, self-opinionated prat,' but he made sure the handset was firmly back on its cradle before he expressed his opinion.

Fairclough was entering the Charge Office at that moment. He looked across to the switchboard and asked what was, for him, an obvious question.

'Vine?'

'Eh?'

'Were you talking about Vine?'

'No. The ACC.'

'Oh.'

'Why Vine?' asked Grafton.

'He's fisted Barstow.'

'Christ! Why?'

'Because he's Vine.'

'Hell's teeth! As if we didn't have enough on our plates.' Grafton raised his eyes in silent prayer. 'Johnny Walker cops it. Blythe gets knifed. We have a crazy ACC who kyboshes the shooters. And just to round everything off, Vine thumps a bloody prisoner. What else can happen?'

'Is that what he says?' Fairclough looked shocked. 'No guns? Even though a copper's been stiffened?'

'That's what he says.'

'He's off his crust!'

'Completely.'

'Does he *know*?'

'He knows, short of drawing him a strip cartoon.'

'Fuller will go ape.'

'Of course. But Fuller isn't a superintendent—'

'What the hell has that to do with it?'

'— therefore Fuller can go ape, bananas, completely crazy. He doesn't carry enough rank for it to matter.'

'Of all the bloody—'

'He can't call out the shooter-boys.'

'And now—' Fairclough blew out his cheeks. 'Now, Vine has to top everything by chucking his weight around.'

'A small thing,' said Grafton drily. 'A thing of no real consequence compared with the cock-up in Audsley Avenue. For me, Constable Vine can suck his own hammer, even if it chokes him. Personally I'd happily see him roast in hell.'

'You think . . .' Fairclough looked strangely uncertain. 'You think I should go to Audsley Avenue? I mean, by this time—'

'I think you should,' interrupted Grafton. 'I think they'll need all the coppers they can get their hands on before they're finished. No guns. So, swamp the place with policemen. What else? That's what I think.'

'Well, no.' Howes moistened his lips and tried again. 'It's, er, y'know. I mean, he's been slashed. Badly. Oh yes, very badly.'

He blinked owlishly, his beard bobbing up and down as he told, in his own near-incomprehensible way, what had happened to Blythe.

WPS Grant sighed and said, 'Eddie, what I want to know is, how badly is he cut? Shall I tell his wife it isn't too serious?'

'We-ell, yes, it's *serious*.' Howes tried not to waffle, but in honesty couldn't help himself. 'I mean, I wouldn't like to have been cut up like that. It's bad. Bad *enough*. Not as bad as Walker, of course.'

'Walker's *dead*, isn't he?'

'Of course.' Howes nodded. 'That's what I mean. Blythe isn't as bad as that.'

'For Christ's sake, Eddie!' pleaded Grant. 'Can't you tell a straight, unvarnished yarn?'

'I'm telling you.' Howes looked offended. 'You want precise details. That's what I'm giving you. He's been badly cut, but not as bad as *all* that.'

'About the face?'

'Yes, of course. About the face. He's stitched and bandaged about the face.'

'And the arm? Somebody mentioned his arm.'

'Of course. I mean, I keep telling you. You won't listen. Face and arm. Stitches and bandaging.'

'How many stitches?'

'I don't know how many stitches, just that he's badly cut. And, oh yes – he said to tell you. Whoever comes. Afro-Caribbean.'

'Eh?'

'The bloke's Afro-Caribbean.'

'Who?'

'The bloke. Y'know. In the house, the bungalow. He didn't recognise him, but what little he saw. Afro-Caribbean, he thinks.'

Grant gazed at Howes in wonder for a moment, then said, 'You're a museum piece, Eddie, I swear. You're not just unusual, you're unique.'

Howes' frown of puzzlement gradually melted into a self-conscious grin, as the thought struck him that he might be being complimented.

He said, 'Thanks. That's nice of you to say so.'

Away from the bungalow – beyond the possible firing-line of anybody taking pot-shots from the windows – Audsley Avenue was beginning to have the appearance of a film set. The cameras were there;

television cameras, of course, hand-held and ready to move into immediate action should anything worth recording happen, but definitely cameras. There wasn't a director, not as such, but a director wasn't needed. This was the raw stuff of life, and the reporters and the commentators more than made up for the lack of a director, by merely being anxious to do their job. The 'extras' were certainly there; the 'crowd scene' people. The good folk of Audsley Avenue were happy, even eager, to tell what they knew about Robert Arkwright.

'. . . and I always found him to be a lovely man. A real gentleman. You couldn't wish for a nicer neighbour . . .'

'. . . so I really don't know. He might have been married. Not now, I don't mean. But one time. He has that look. That sad, lost look they all have, when . . .'

'. . . and well, no, I don't know where he is. On his holidays somewhere. That's all I know. He kept himself to himself, y'know. Maybe a bit stuck up. Didn't join in the local festivities. He wasn't one for socialising . . .'

They each told all they knew. Unfortunately, none of them knew very much.

The 'supporting cast' were there. The police officers – a very impressive 'supporting cast' – standing guard and keeping as many people away from the bungalow as possible. Sitting in squad cars, listening out for any instructions that might come from somebody who knew what the hell was happening, or what the hell was going to happen. Looking as intelligent as possible while being bored out of their respective skulls by the inactivity. Whiling away the time by talking quietly among themselves.

'. . . And anyway, do we know who he is?'

'Some lunatic who doesn't like the Bill.'

'Who does, these days?'

'That's a fact, too.'

94

'They tell me he's sliced old Blythe up something shocking.'

'Aye. That's what I hear.'

'Ah, but Blythe will get better. Poor old Walker won't.'

'Whoever's in there is an absolute bastard.'

'Too true. He wants hanging up by the balls to dry.'

'Naw. He'll get away with it.'

'Eh?'

'Some funny farmer will explain why it's all because he wasn't given a proper rattle when he was a kid.'

'Let me have elbow room, boy. I'd give him a bloody rattle.'

A detective constable, not having been told what to do next, jerked his head and remarked, 'The gaffer seems to be winding himself up for something.'

A squad car officer growled, 'The sequence, see? First we try to talk him out. Then, if that doesn't work, we turn nasty.'

And, indeed, Fuller was 'winding himself up'. He slammed the receiver back onto the rest of the handset and poked a forefinger into the dialing hole again.

'Pardon me, Inspector.' The oldster, Gowan, the one-time Hong Kong Chief Superintendent, cleared his throat apologetically and continued, 'Has he hung up on you?'

'Three times.' Fuller's annoyance showed in his tone. 'Three times he's answered, then . . .'

'There's no need to dial,' said Gowan gently. 'Just the bungalow telephone, that's all it's connected to. Just turn the handle. That's all it needs.'

'Oh!'

'Have you done this sort of thing before?' asked Gowan.

'No.' Fuller's answer was terse. 'Never.'

'Don't.' Gowan dropped a hand and interrupted

95

Fuller's reach for the handset handle. 'He'll only hang up on you again.'

'All right.' Fuller lifted his hand from the telephone set. Those first two words were tight and hard then, like a spring uncoiling, his tone became softer and more desperate. He said, 'Look, Mr Gowan. I am, as you reminded me a couple of hours ago, only an Inspector. A straightforward thieving job, a break-in, a rape, even a no-nonsense murder, I can handle them. I have handled them. No sweat. But this is different. This isn't detective work. This is a siege. There's a woman – a Mrs Littlewood, the cleaning lady – who isn't accounted for. She might be in there with him. She might be alive. She might be dead. We don't *know*. But I'm expected to make certain decisions.' Fuller took a deep breath then continued, 'I'll take every decision I'm expected to take and beyond, but the truth is, this situation needs rank that I don't carry. This one needs top brass. Far too many people can crowd me off the face of the earth if I take a wrong step. Can, and will!' He paused, passed his tongue across dry lips, then ended, 'The truth is, I'm scared. A *lot* scared.'

'Of your job? Of being sacked?'

'Christ, no! Of making that mad bastard in there do something crazy. Of saying the wrong thing. Of not saying the right thing. Of upsetting the whole apple-cart by being too ham-fisted. If the Littlewood woman is in there, and if she's still alive, I could kill her, literally. Merely by saying the wrong words.'

'By taking things in too much of a hurry,' said Gowan gently.

'Just that.' Fuller nodded his head. 'It's a king-sized responsibility. Too big a responsibility for a mere inspector.'

'A psychiatrist?' suggested Gowan.

Fuller murmured, 'God help us!'

'You are,' said Gowan calmly, 'doing things the wrong way. You're allowing him to make you worry. You should be concentrating on making him worry.'

Fuller looked puzzled.

'You're annoyed – upset, perhaps – because he hangs up every time you ring,' explained Gowan. 'But he hangs up because he *can* hang up. Because he knows you'll ring again. He hangs up because, in his primitive little mind, he has it all worked out. You'll stay at the telephone and he'll know where you are. To an extent he's able to control you. But,' and Gowan's gentle smile wasn't really gentle, 'he's also waiting for you to ring. You're the only link he has with the outside world. Without realising it, he wants you to ring. He wants to know you're still here. He wants to be able to hang up on you, again and again and again. In effect, he wants to control the telephone link. That way, he thinks he'll be able to work out some arrangement with you eventually. At his speed. A way to get out of this mess he's in. To outsmart the police. Understand?'

Fuller took a deep breath, then blew out his cheeks before he said, 'I think so. It's involved. If it's like you say it is—'

'It is, Inspector. With minor variations, it's always like that.'

'So?'

'We take charge. We decide when we're going to make use of the telephone link. We make him wait.'

'What if he—'

'You can only be reasonably sure of what a man does, or what he's likely to do, when that man's locked away in a police cell. While he's on the loose, it's always a matter of calculated guesswork.'

'You hit things.' Fuller allowed himself a wry smile. 'That must be said. You hit some very uncomfortable buttons.'

'I've been there,' Gowan reminded him gently. 'I know how it feels. But I can give you some advice.'

'Why not?'

'Leave things for a while. Let it simmer. Let the man inside sweat a little. *You* set the pace. And, until you want to go into overdrive, it's always slower than he wants.'

The Reverend Reginald Palfrey, BA, was lying in his teeth and he knew it. He frowned his misery at the wall of the vicarage study as he talked into the mouthpiece of the telephone.

'James, I know you're not well, I know you're retired, but I'm at my wits' end. Family Eucharist starts in little more than half an hour and I don't think I can take it.'

The James he was talking to asked why, and Palfrey continued to lie.

'I think it's something I've eaten. With Angela away, I seem to be taking snacks when and where I can. I think it must be that. Something I've eaten.'

There was a short silence while the James at the other end of the telephone link-up spoke. Then Palfrey closed his eyes for a moment, as if in relief, and ended the conversation.

'That's good of you, James. If I can take the day off, perhaps get some fresh air into my lungs, then pamper myself a little and lie down for a couple of hours this afternoon. And if you'll take the services for the rest of the day . . . It really is most kind of you.'

## 0845 Hours

Rogate-on-Sands Memorial Hospital was not one of those massive, umpteen-hundred-beds, miles-and-miles-of-corridors jobs. It was, in effect, Tom Tiddler's

Ground where all the local medics tried out a few stitching jobs, or a spot of minor surgery here and there. There was a staff, of course, and a few tiny wards. There were even visiting specialists. But in the main it was a scoop-net for run-of-the-mill ailments, broken bones and the end products of motor-cars nudging each other at high speed.

It was a cosy place, despite its gloomy, red-brick exterior and its tiny, rhododendron-strangled grounds. It smelled of Mansion Polish and Lysol. Its composition floors sparkled and its walls gave off the dull, deep reflection of a good class, silk-finish paint. It had large-bladed ceiling fans whose steadily circling sur-faces cooled the air on this mountingly hot Sunday.

It also had some very friendly ward sisters who, when they weren't rushing around making the rubber soles of their shoes squeak, were happy to share a cuppa and a cigarette with equally friendly members of the local constabulary.

And it must be noted that, when necessary, Detective Sergeant Wragg could be uncommonly friendly.

'And he's still in there, is he?' The ward sister's eyes were wide with excited interest. 'Still in the bungalow?'

'Oh aye.'

'The man who's killed Mr Walker and slashed Sergeant Blythe?'

'That's the one. He's still in there.' Wragg screwed up his face and scowled determined vengeance. He growled, 'And when he comes *out*—'

'What?'

'That's when all the debts are going to be collected.'

The ward sister nodded understandingly, and Wragg sipped newly brewed tea appreciatively.

Wragg, of course, should not have been in the ward sister's office. Wragg should have been in Audsley Avenue. Fuller had given very strict instructions:

99

everybody to be moved from houses within shooting range of Number Twenty-Six. But (an opinion long held by Wragg) Fuller was something of a wet dab. Indeed, very much a wet dab.

Detective Sergeant James Wragg shared his own candid opinion with the ward sister.

He said, 'The Inspector's a bit of a wet dab.'

'Is he?'

'Sunny Jim should have been slung out of that bungalow some time ago.'

'Really?'

'That's what I'd have done. It's what I would have done if Fuller hadn't stopped me.'

'But he has a knife, hasn't he?'

'He has a blade,' agreed Wragg. He hesitated, then made up his mind and in a stagey, off-hand tone added, 'We think he has a gun, too.'

'A gun!'

'It's possible.'

'Good heavens!'

Again, Wragg sipped the tea. It was, as he'd expected, very good tea. Not at all like the slop served out to the patients. It was very nice tea and very nice company; a good deal better than the company of Fuller, Tidy and the silly old duffer Fuller seemed to be intimidated by. It had (Wragg decided) been a good idea to move from centre-stage for a while, to slide behind the wheel of his car and nip off for a quick cup of tea at the Memorial.

'Will there . . . ' The ward sister hesitated, then asked, 'Will the police have guns? Will there be shooting?'

'I would think so. It shouldn't have been necessary, of course. But it is *now*, and what it's likely to develop into is anybody's guess. Fuller's lost control of things.'

It took a little more than fifteen minutes for Wragg to drink the tea. It was a very pleasant fifteen minutes, during which time he exaggerated slightly, preened

100

himself a little and glowed comfortably in the warmth of the ward sister's feminine wiles and gentle mock-amazement. It was the usual catch-'em-while-they're-showing-off routine and, as always, the poor guy hadn't a chance.

They strolled side-by-side from the ward sister's office to the main entrance of the Memorial Hospital. Wragg felt at least ten feet tall and growing fast. The ward sister silently congratulated herself; with a modicum of luck she'd wrangled herself an evening's entertainment in the company of, and at the expense of, a moderately good-looking police officer who (from all remarks and external appearances) wasn't already earmarked for the altar, and (which was more important) hadn't obviously wandered down some aisle in the past.

They reached the Reception Desk.

The receptionist was saying, 'No, I'm sorry. We have no record of an accident, and we have no record of a Mrs Littlewood having been admitted. I think your best bet would be to contact the police.'

The man at the Reception Desk looked worried, but smiled and said, 'Thanks.'

'The police should know,' said the receptionist. 'If she's had an accident, she might have been taken to another hospital.'

'Thanks,' said the man again.

The man left the Reception Desk and left the hospital immediately in front of Wragg and the ward sister.

He was wearing a royal blue track-suit, with a red stripe down the sides of the trousers and the sleeves.

Constable Tidy had been on the spot from the very beginning. He'd pulled Walker's body clear, then done what he could to stop Blythe bleeding to death before the ambulance arrived. If this particular shambles was anybody's incident – dog dirt and all – it was Jim Tidy's.

101

But, because he was Tidy, he'd kept in the background as much as possible. He'd watched and listened, sometimes with approval, sometimes with a degree of dismay, but now, with the disappearance of Wragg and with Fuller on his way to Divisional Headquarters, determined to scorch the ears off the Assistant Chief Constable via a closed-line telephone link with Force Headquarters, Tidy felt very much on his own. He was not the senior officer at the scene, but he was senior enough to be expected to carry messy babies. He was also the senior of the Rogate-on-Sands coppers at the scene. And it *was* his incident.

It did not help that he looked a mess. The blood on his tunic and down the front of his trousers had darkened and soaked into the material, but it had not yet crusted. It was sticky and mildly disgusting to the touch. The tips of his fingers were smeared with the stuff. He'd lost his peaked cap in the mêlée at the rear door of the bungalow; it had fallen off his head and had been trampled underfoot. Since then he'd run his fingers through his hair a few times and, as well as soiling his greying thatch, he'd also left hints of smear marks high on his forehead.

And now the realisation of his present grubbiness reminded him that he hadn't switched the hot water system to automatic at his home in Finehead.

A small thing, when placed alongside the dog's breakfast in Audsley Avenue, a comparatively unimportant thing, but one of the tiny day-to-day details which reminded him of Madge. Had she been around – had she been at home – hot water would have been waiting. A soak in a steaming bath, followed by a brisk rub-down with fresh, clean towels.

Those were part of the luxury of marriage to a good woman. They'd been taken for granted when they'd been available but, by God, they were missed, and their

102

value was re-assessed when they were no longer there.

A voice said, 'You look worried, Constable.'

Tidy turned his head, smiled at Gowan and said, 'Not worried, sir. A touch of self-indulgence, perhaps.'

'Self-indulgence?'

'Actually, self-pity.'

Gowan returned the smile and said, 'I'm sorry.'

'I think it's the lack of action,' explained Tidy. 'Just standing here, waiting, gives you time to think. Time to indulge in things like self-pity.'

'Your Inspector seems to have left.'

'He has priorities away from here at the moment.'

'Unusual, but a nice change.' Gowan gave the ghost of a nod of approval. He added, 'Loyalty, especially in the Police Service. The usual thing is a continual criticism of those in authority, with or without reason.'

'I'm sorry. I don't—'

Tidy's reply was cut short by the ring of the temporary telephone. Both Tidy and Gowan instinctively reached out a hand to pick up the handset. They both stopped midway. Tidy hesitated, then waved a hand for Gowan to take the call.

Gowan picked up the receiver, stayed silent for about ten slow heartbeats, then spoke in a distinctly genteel and slightly high-pitched accent.

'Hello. I beg your pardon? I'm sorry, I don't understand. I'm sorry.' Then in a terse, annoyed tone, 'You must have the wrong number.'

As he replaced the receiver his eyes held the twinkle of barely concealed delight.

Tidy waited.

'He doesn't know,' explained Gowan. 'We have an edge. Whichever number he dials, he ends up here. That's the way it's worked. He hasn't tumbled yet. With luck, he won't. It's an advantage. Our advantage. And we use whatever advantage we can get.'

103

Tidy continued to wait.

'I've done this a few times,' said Gowan. 'The man inside the bungalow; I now know what his voice is like. He doesn't know what my voice is like. One more slight edge.'

'Oh!'

'Furthermore – think about it – *he's* telephoned. He thought he'd dialed the police station. At a guess, that took some doing. It must have. It's proof that he's worried. He's also made a deliberate decision, to contact the police. In his position, that means he's worried. The penny's dropped. He's starting to realise what a mess he's in. He wants to find if there's a way out. And now he has another, additional worry.' Gowan's lips moved into a quick, mirthless smile. 'Can he contact the police? Whatever he wants, whatever scheme he cooks up, can he let people know? Let the police know? This time it's just a wrong number. That's what he thinks. Perhaps his finger found the wrong hole in the dial. The wrong button. And next time? We deliberately make him panic a little. Whatever he wants to do, whatever he *decides* to do, he can't do it. That first dialling was the break-through. From here on, dialling will be comparatively easy, but it won't get him anywhere. We'll see to that. Wrong numbers. Engaged lines. Anything, until *we're* ready to talk. The trick the police have to pull is to get him frustrated enough to have him ripping the phone from its socket.'

'Neat,' murmured Tidy.

'Not neat. Difficult, difficult and dangerous. Like juggling broken glass.'

Tolby talked *sotto voce* to the man from the local radio station.

'There's a lunatic inside the bungalow. Number Twenty-Six.'

'A lunatic? A real lunatic?'

'Not a certified nutter. Not that. But I'm told he's killed one copper and, by the sound of things, fatally wounded another. That's what I'm told. That sort of a lunatic.'

'Christ!'

'Now he's in there, defying them to go in and get him.'

'Is that official?'

'Official?'

'Y'know, can I use it? Where did you get the information?'

'Hey, hold off, friend.' Tolby raised warning eyebrows. 'I get my information. I do you a personal favour by passing enough on to point you in the general direction, but that's all. You do your own checking. And you do your own groundwork for the background stuff.'

'The old boy.' The man from the local radio station gestured towards Gowan. 'The divisional Sultan of Fuzz?'

'No.'

'From Top Office?'

'I've never seen him around before.'

'Must be.'

'If you say so. Just don't quote *me*.'

'Tolby, old son.' There were hurt feelings in the tone. 'I've done you favours before today.'

'Is that a fact?'

'So don't just sit around and watch me drop one.'

'Would I? Would I be such an unnaturally ungrateful individual, after all those favours you've done *me*?'

Crosby took a taxi home. His car was firmly attached to a lamp standard on C Beat. Constable Wood was painstakingly taking statements from witnesses at the scene. The ambulance had delivered Crosby to the Memorial Hospital and the Accident and Emergency types had examined the pigeon's-egg-sized lump above his eyebrow before handing him a handful of glorified aspirins and advising him to check with his own medic. By that time the ambulance had returned to its depot and the only means of transport available seemed to be the duo of cabs parked at the hospital rank.

He paid the taxi, walked up the loose gravel of the tiny drive with a vaguely drunken gait and let himself into the house he'd left more than two hours previously.

Crosby was a middle-aged man. He was a police officer, a very senior police officer; a uniformed Superintendent. All this, but he wasn't too far from tears as the great bore of self-pity threatened to overwhelm him.

His wife hurried into the hall from the kitchen. She saw his pale, unhappy face, with the bruise on the forehead. She saw the dishevelled and dust-marked uniform. She hurried towards him with outstretched hands.

She almost sobbed, 'Andrew! Have you been attacked?'

'Attacked?'

'Has somebody—'

'Oh no. No.' Crosby caught at one of her hands and held it close to his upper arm. 'I've had an accident. With the car.'

'An accident? You mean somebody ran into you?'

'No, not that.'

'I don't understand. How have you—'

'I hit a lamp standard.' He choked as he tried to swallow, then he allowed his voice to break as he repeated, '*I hit a bloody lamp standard.*'

'Why? I mean, what made you—'

'I'm sorry. Forget it.' A fat, heartbroken tear trickled

106

down each of his cheeks. 'I've been made to look a fool, that's all. I think I might have written off the car. There's a chance I might end up in court, facing a Driving Without Due Consideration charge. And . . .' He gazed at her through moist eyes. 'And I'm no damn good. That's about the size of it. No good to the force. No good to you. No good to anybody.'

'And that's a stupid thing to say.' Her voice was firm but gentle. 'What does that make me? A woman silly enough to marry a no-good man?'

'I'm sorry, but—'

'They've been telephoning for you.'

'Who?'

'The office. They've phoned a couple of times.'

'Did they say what—'

'It doesn't matter. I'll ring back and tell them to contact Chief Inspector Forester.'

'He's away in Tenerife, I think. He's on leave.'

'It doesn't matter. I'll tell them to contact Fuller.' She was gently guiding him towards the stairs. 'Now you get undressed while I run you a bath. Then to bed, while I get your uniform ready for drycleaning. Then we'll get the doctor out. You're a sick man, Andrew. You're in no condition to make decisions.'


## 0900 Hours

Fuller was in his office at Rogate-on-Sands Divisional Headquarters. He was seated behind his desk. He was holding the handset of his office telephone in one hand, and the look of sheer disbelief on his face bordered on the comical. There was perhaps a tiny tremble of the hand holding the telephone. Partly due to the increasing grip and partly due to Fuller's mighty great effort to keep calm.

'You – ' He cleared his throat then, in a slightly steadier tone, said, 'You do realise the situation here, sir?'

'What you've told me, Inspector.' The Assistant Chief Constable's voice was as calmly precise and as pompously correct as ever. 'I have to take certain things on trust, of course.'

'Sir?'

'That your assessment has a certain validity. That, I fear, is one of the things I have to take on trust.'

'An officer's been murdered.'

'He's dead, Fuller. Further than that we mustn't go without a coroner's verdict.'

'Good God!'

'You may be right, of course—'

'Well, thank *you*, sir.'

'— but please don't base your reports on personal conjecture.'

'Sir.' Fuller's eyes stared. 'A man's dead, one of *our* men. He didn't have a heart attack. He wasn't run down by a bus. His throat was opened up.'

'I fail to see—'

'A uniformed sergeant has sustained terrible injuries. He's cut badly about the face and arms. He may, of course, have done it while shaving, but—'

'Watch it, Inspector. Have a care.'

'*Watch it!*'

'This is not a joking matter.'

'No, sir. I am not joking.'

'Whatever's happened, Fuller, whatever's happened, you can't justify a firearms team against one man armed only with a knife.'

'And that, sir, is a load of ballocks, even when delivered from your chair.'

'Fuller, I don't like your tone. It is a highly insolent tone. An offensive tone. It shows scant respect for the

108

difference in our rank.'

'No respect at all, sir.'

'What?'

'I have no respect for a man who hides behind convenient rules and regulations, regardless of circumstances. Regardless of who gets hurt. Regardless of who's been hurt. Regardless of who's been *killed*.'

'Inspector, how dare you—'

'I dare, sir. Without much of an effort, I dare. And before you start dreaming of what you might do to me, of the discipline you're going to mete out, give your imagination a free run of the possibilities as far as the press is concerned. The Police Chief who refused to bend the rules a little, even to save a life. Imagine the headlines. Imagine the fancy questions likely to be asked in Parliament. The even fancier answers *you* might be required to provide. 'I "dare", sir. But, I wonder, dare you?'

Fuller didn't wait for a reply. He lowered the receiver and laid it across its prongs. He lowered it gently, as if the plastic was as brittle as spun sugar.

He allowed his hand to rest on the telephone lightly and without pressure while he gazed, out of focus, at the closed door of the office and contemplated what he had just done.

It was (he supposed) a matter of principles. He should have felt proud. Pleased with himself. Gratified that he'd had the simple guts to stand up for that in which be believed. But he wasn't.

Principles!

This bloody job didn't run to principles. Ask Stalker.

John Stalker, one-time Deputy Chief Constable of the Manchester outfit. He'd had principles by the bucketful. By the ton.

If ever a man could carry corn!

But it hadn't done much good. Some secret (and,

maybe, not so secret) bastard had crept up behind and slit open the sack. And all the corn had drained away, and poor old Stalker had been left there, holding an empty sack and looking a little stupid.

As easy as that. As simple as that.

So-o, ask Stalker; he'll tell you how much weight principles carry.

The civilian clerk was late. This was not unusual enough to knock the earth off its axis. Indeed, had Stan Carter not been at least a little late, and especially on a Sunday, somebody, somewhere might have been tempted to raise a standard on some forgotten flagpole. And, as always, as he walked into the Charge Office, he looked over his shoulder at the wall clock and expressed his usual make-believe surprise.

'Good God! It's not *that* time, is it?'

'As near as dammit,' countered Grafton.

'I wouldn't have thought.'

'Vine's in.' Grafton got down to business with unusual alacrity. 'Barstow had a skinful last night.'

'Barstow again?'

'Bail him, as soon as you like.'

'Will do.'

'I've already filled in the bail forms.'

'Good.'

'He's been knocked about a bit.'

'Eh! Who?'

'Barstow. I think Vine's hammered him, but he won't say.'

'Who?'

'Barstow. He says he fell. But that's all ballocks, of course.'

'Why should he—'

'Just handle with care. That's all. No loose questions. Otherwise, if the nasty stuff starts flying around some

110

might stick to your fingers.'

'Oh! Ah, yes. Just so. Just so.'

Carter favoured clip-on bow-ties. They were usually the colour of cheap port wine. Combined with his girth and his shiny pate, they gave him the appearance of a stand-up comic. One of the boom-boom school of comedians, complete with near-the-knuckle one-liners. Even the way he walked, the spring and the bounce, added to the illusion. Until he opened his mouth, that is. It then became very obvious. He lacked any sense of fun. In the let's-have-a-quick-chuckle stakes he was well behind either Vine or Wood, and that was going some!

As he unclipped the tie, he said, 'Fuller's car is in the park.'

'He's in his office.'

'Ah.'

'Purchasing cost-price fertiliser from the Assistant Chief.'

'Eh? What's he want fert—' The penny dropped and Carter allowed a near-obligatory grin to bend his lips for a split second. 'Oh,' he lied, 'I see.'

But the truth was, he didn't see and he continued to look vaguely puzzled. He opened the cheap, pressed-cardboard attaché case he'd brought with him, dropped the bow-tie into it and at the same time took out a Thermos jug. He walked to an ancient green steel filing cabinet in a corner of the Charge Office, slid the bottom drawer out, then carefully stored the attaché case and the upright Thermos jug out of sight.

Grafton, who was blessed with a natural sense of timing, murmured, 'John Walker's dead.'

'What? Y'mean he died last—'

'He died this morning. Some evil sod slit his throat.'

Carter's eyes widened.

'The same evil sod cut Blythe into salami slices.'

'Jesus!' Carter looked dazed as he pushed the drawer

111

of the filing cabinet closed.

'Yeah. Fairclough has had a mad arsonist to deal with, and there's a donkey in the dog pound.' Then, in a deliberately throw-away tone, he ended, 'Other than that, it's been a quiet morning so far.'

The telephone bell rang again. Tidy moved a hand but Gowan shook his head and smiled.

'Don't answer,' he advised.

'I don't see—'

'We can only play "wrong number" so many times. Once is enough for now. Let Telecom take the strain this time.'

'Hoping *he* doesn't disconnect us all in a fit of pique.'

'That's always a possibility,' agreed Gowan.

Tidy stared at the rear door of the bungalow for a few moments, then asked, 'Your opinion, please. Will he come out?'

'Spin a coin.' Gowan moved a shoulder.

'You've had experience of these situations.' It sounded almost like an accusation, as if Tidy suspected Gowan of keeping secret an outcome he already knew.

'They're all different. There's a general pattern, but when the details arrive they're all different.'

'That's no help.'

'Let's assume we get guns. Let's assume we can convince him we won't blow his head off the moment he shows it.'

'Then?'

'He might come out.'

The bell was still ringing. It seemed to be going on forever. Tidy felt like pushing fingers into his ears in an attempt to stop the torment.

'And if we don't get guns?' he asked.

'Has he got a gun?' countered Gowan. Then, 'I understand it's a possibility.'

'It's a possibility,' agreed Tidy.

'If he has, and if we haven't, he might think he can shoot his way out.'

'He might just be right,' said Tidy grimly.

'That's defeatist talk, Constable!' Gowan was mildly critical.

'Yeah. That's the way I feel at the moment. Defeatist.'

The bell stopped ringing, and the silence seemed thick and unnatural.

Some of the holiday-makers were starting to leave the hotels and the guest houses. They sported thin cotton frocks and open-necked, short-sleeved shirts. Because it was Rogate-on-Sands, and not Blackpool, or Morecambe, or Margate, or Brighton, they settled themselves on the benches in Rock Walk, or on the Promenade, opened their books, their magazines and their newspapers and prepared themselves for the morning barbecue. Come evening, their skins would be deep pink, moving towards scarlet, but the anguish of slowly grilling flesh would be almost exquisite – and that, too, would be part of their holiday and proof of their holiday; not to return home sunburned would be tantamount to admitting they'd had a poor holiday.

And perhaps an hour or so from now their eyes would become drowsy, and they'd put their books, their magazines, their newspapers to one side and they'd cat-nap for a while. And because their sense of sight was not being used, their sense of hearing would become more acute. The background noise would gradually impose itself and wrap itself around an already warm relaxation like a cosy, audible eiderdown.

Fine. That was the Great British Summer Holiday. That was Rogate-on-Sands.

But Audsley Avenue was also part of Rogate-on-Sands, and what was happening in Audsley Avenue was

113

in no way part of the Great British Summer Holiday.

## *0915 Hours*

It had seemed so easy.

Almost four hours ago, when he'd first realised that his wife and his brother had shared the same bed that night, it would have been easy. Or (to be strictly accurate) it *might* have been easy. Daniels wasn't too sure about anything any more.

He *could* have walked away.

He *could* have upped sticks, packed a suitcase, slipped his chequebook into his pocket, drawn every penny from their joint account, then caught a train to somewhere beyond the far horizon.

Or could he?

That had been his intention; to wait until the bank opened, then leave her to sort things out on her own. Not with Chris. For Christ's sake, not with Chris. Chris wouldn't have even acknowledged her existence. He knew Chris well enough to know that.

And, okay; maybe that was as much as she deserved.

On the other hand . . .

He knew Chris well enough to know a lot of other things, too. His way with women; the undoubted fact that, when she'd switched from Chris to himself, Beth was already very much 'soiled goods'. So-o, having been honest enough to face up to that certainty, why was he getting so up-tight because she'd slipped a gear just this once?

Just this once?

How did he know that, either?

Charlie Daniels had always prided himself on being a calm, logical type. No sweat. No exaggeration. In the force, when he was making out a report or giving

114

evidence in court, he told only the unvarnished truth. No touching things up. No 'verbals'. No general fannying around. Just what was, not what he'd like it to be.

And that was it. The two-and-two-are-four outlook. Beth and Chris had spent the night together. Beth was his wife. Chris was his brother. Those were the facts, period.

So now he could either forget it, or do something.

But what?

For the first time in his basically insignificant life, Charlie Daniels faced a fundamental truth about himself. He was not a 'do something' sort of bloke. The soft option was his natural choice. It always had been. He could argue, back to front, until he was just about ready to crawl up his own anus, anything to get out of a course of action likely to upset his own personal apple-cart.

He was, of course, a prat. He was an easy-way-out-sort-of-a-prat – an amiable sort of a prat who disliked rocking boats but, without a shadow of a doubt, a fully-paid-up-member of the Society of Complete Prats.

As with Beth. As with Chris. Don't make waves; don't rock the boat; accept life for what it is and be satisfied to live it. It was, when all was said and done, the old slice-off-a-cut-cake situation. Nothing new. Nothing novel. Moreover, this particular cake had had a slice or two removed before he'd popped it into his own personal oven. Nothing surer. With Chris sniffing around, bet on it.

It was the way of the world, and very much the way of the present-day world.

Daniels had left the house to walk the streets. Not to go anywhere, merely to think. To reach what he was pleased to call 'conclusions'. To 'come to terms'. In effect, to figure out the easy option.

115

Between friends, eh? Between brothers. A little cross-banging, and Beth hadn't denied it. She hadn't lied, not really. And at the present moment she was wetting those easily removable panties of hers. She was thinking he'd done what he'd threatened to do. What – to be honest, and on the spur of the moment – he'd intended to do until he'd cooled off and come to his senses.

To walk out of her life. To make the grand and final exit. To call at the bank and withdraw every penny of their joint account. To catch a train to somewhere and do a complete vanishing trick. Then to start a new life.

That's what she'd expected, what she *still* expected, and although she hadn't fought or argued, or even voiced any real complaint, that lower lip of hers had trembled a little. And for real. Not a put-on. The possible outcome of what she'd done had risen to the surface of her consciousness, and frightened the crap out of her.

Okay, maybe he should have done it.

It was what could have happened. What would have happened in a book, or on a film. That or a long drawn-out divorce palaver. Unlimited hassle. Wagon-loads full of worry. And, of course, the shovelling of hard-earned cash into the pockets of various solicitors.

Fortunately for all concerned, Daniels had come to his senses. He'd come off the boil, cooled down from the original simmer.

He smiled wryly to himself as he came to the street corner. He rounded the corner and collided with Palfrey, who was rounding the corner from the other direction. They each caught the other's arms, staggered slightly, then recognised each other.

'Vicar!'

'Constable Daniels.'

'I'm sorry.'

116

'Not at all. I was just as much to blame.'

It was one of those swish four-star sea-front hotels. The windows of the dining room, the lounge bar, the sun lounge and one of the smaller conference rooms looked out across the prom and Rock Walk and over the Irish Sea. Every inch of floor-space was wall-to-wall carpeted. Every public room was a poem of chandeliers, table-lamps, wall-lights, polished mahogany, shining brass and gleaming oak. The staff were all handsomely uniformed. The flower arrangements were immaculate.

It was a very swish four-star hotel and, at the end of a stay there, the departing guest was presented with a very swish four-star bill.

The manageress of this hotel said, 'It must be serious.' They were in her office, and she was fishing for information as she stood up from her desk and, very deliberately, pulled down and locked the roll-top.

'It's serious,' agreed Grant.

'I know her husband's a policeman.'

'A sergeant, actually.'

'She's a quiet lady. She doesn't talk much.'

'Not like some people.'

'I'm sorry.' The manageress bridled. 'I shouldn't—'

'*I'm* sorry.' And Grant meant it. This damn detail was getting at her. She and Police Constable Yates had deliberately entered the hotel via the tradesman's entrance, and had been careful not to go anywhere where they might be seen from the reception desk. It had been a little like playing puss-in-the-corner, and Grant hadn't liked it too much. She gave a tiny little cough and said, 'Sergeant Blythe's been injured.'

'Oh!' The manageress sounded genuinely sorry and a little embarrassed when she said, 'I didn't know.'

'How could you?'

'No, but—'

117

'I know what you mean.' Grant's tone gentled slightly. 'Forget it. This isn't an easy job. We need your help.'

'Yes, of course.' Then curiosity got the upper hand again, and the manageress added, 'Is it bad? Critical? Is he likely to die?'

'It's not fatal, not even likely to be fatal. But he'll carry some very bad scars on his face. And his arm.'

'Oh dear.'

Grant hesitated, then asked, 'How might she take it?'

'What?' The manageress looked startled.

'I don't know her. You do. What might we expect in the way of reaction?'

'She usually has her inhaler handy, so—'

'Her what?'

'Her inhaler. She suffers from asthma. Asthma, and chronic bronchitis. If she gets too upset or excited, she needs her inhaler. It's a sort of puffer, a small, aerosol thing she has to—'

'I know what you mean.'

'She's—' The manageress creased her forehead. She wanted to help, but didn't want to over-state. She said, 'She's not ill. I'm not suggesting that. Not disabled, in any way. She's a delightful person. Well liked. But, y'know, if she's really upset, it sometimes tends to—'

'Thank you.' WPS Grant stepped in and put the manageress out of her misery. 'We'll bear in mind what you've said. Now I hope you'll be available, if we need you. Somebody she knows. That's the main thing.'

Audsley Avenue had undergone a remarkable meta-morphosis. In the course of a couple of hours or so, it had changed from a dreary, moderately well-off part of the town into a highly charged, strangely exciting place. Murder had been committed. A uniformed police sergeant had been savagely knifed. The place was crawling with coppers and media people. The

118

atmosphere was gradually building up to an almost electric apprehension.

Those who'd seen the sharp end of Hitler's War recognised the feeling. Like the positioning of troops prior to a set-piece battle. Like the assembling of flyers in a briefing room prior to the take-off on a bombing operation.

The locals watched and chatted quietly together.

The pensioner, who'd once been a Captain in a tank regiment, said, 'A little like the run-up to Overlord. Don't you think?'

The pensioner who'd once been a Major in the Parachute Regiment touched his clipped moustache and replied, 'Those villagers, eh? They all gave us a damned good time, though. Made the waiting very tolerable.'

The ex-Captain observed, 'We certainly arsed up their lanes with all that equipment.'

'And the Yanks, of course. Don't forget the Yanks.'

'Who can ever forget the Yanks?'

'Like this.' The ex-Major touched his moustache again. 'Much like this, don't you know. Stiffening up the sinews and summoning up the blood. That sort of thing.'

A motor-patrol Sergeant wandered closer and proffered advice.

He said, 'You'd be well advised to stay indoors, gentlemen.' With his left hand he removed the peaked cap from his head. With his right hand he pulled a handkerchief from his trouser pocket. He wiped the sweat-band of the peaked cap as he continued, 'There's a distinct possibility of some shooting, I'm afraid.'

'I've been told,' said the ex-Captain.

'And we're *not*,' snapped the ex-Major.

'Eh?' The motor-patrol Sergeant blinked.

'Afraid,' amplified the ex-Major. 'We've both been under fire. *Real* fire. More than once.'

'Oh, very droll.' The Sergeant replaced both cap and

119

handkerchief. 'You must tell me when you're going to do your next funny act.'

'The commissioned officers?' asked the ex-Captain. 'Where are they?'

'The what?'

'The commissioned officers.'

'The commissioned officers?'

'You know.' The ex-Captain moved his hand in a vague but all-embracing gesture. 'The superintendents, or whatever they're called. Where are they?'

'No commissioned ranks in the police, sir. We all do the same job, more or less.'

'Don't talk complete cock, man.' The ex-Major had a very short fuse. '*Somebody* makes decisions, what? PC bloody Plod is only there to do what he's told to do.'

Before the motor-patrol Sergeant could answer, the ex-Captain said, 'You're a non-com, of course—'

'Salt of the earth, the non-coms,' growled the ex-Major.

'—so I presume you're in charge, pending the arrival of some officer.'

'Not me.' The Sergeant shook his head.

'Dammit, you hold the rank. Use it.'

'I'm Road Traffic,' explained the Sergeant. 'I'm not even foot patrol, much less CID. I'm not expected – not even *allowed* – to handle this sort of a situation.'

'Quite right, eh?' The ex-Major jerked his head in approval. 'You don't expect an Intelligence wallah to know anything about gun-laying. Same thing.'

They all three turned their heads as they heard the ring of the telephone.

The ex-Major muttered, 'You can tell by the sound of the damned thing. A field telephone. Bloody useless. You can't trust 'em. Bog full of bloody gremlins.'

120

# 0930 Hours

It was nice and cool between the sheets. His wife had drawn the curtains against the glare of the morning sun and the springs of the expensive mattress made it feel as if he were suspended in air. The bedroom was clean and sweet-smelling. And he had a good wife.

The realisation hit him quite suddenly. He had a good wife, a damn good wife, and he didn't appreciate her.

Crosby murmured, 'I don't really think I need a doctor, dear.'

'Better to be safe.' His wife touched the pillow near his head. 'If it's slight concussion, it can have after-effects.'

'It is Sunday.'

'He'll be out before noon. That's what they say.'

'Look, it's not that I—'

'Andrew!' There was make-believe crossness in his wife's tone. 'Be a good patient, please. I know there's nothing serious, but a doctor should check you over, just to be sure.'

Tidy approached the handset when the telephone bell rang. Then he stopped, glanced at Gowan and motioned towards the telephone with a tiny nod of his head.

'You?' he suggested.

'I may come unstuck,' said Gowan.

'The same with anybody,' said Tidy heavily. 'But at least you have some past experience.'

'I'll do my best.' The telephone was into its fourth ring when Gowan picked up the receiver and said, 'Hello.'

'Who's that?' The voice was deep and held just a

121

touch of breathlessness.

'I know who that is.' Gowan's tone was both steady and friendly. 'Shall we start on a firm basis?'

'What's that?'

'Shall we exchange identities?'

'Hey, man, you a cop?'

'Of course,' lied Gowan.

'You hold rank? Real rank?'

'Yes.'

'I want out of here.'

'Naturally.'

'I mean *out*, man.'

'That's why you rang, surely?'

'No slammer. You got that? Don't you start talking about the slammer.'

'We negotiate,' said Gowan quietly.

'Hey, copper, you're smooth. You don't mean that.'

'Oh yes.'

'You don't mean that, no way.'

'We negotiate,' repeated Gowan. 'You can't stay in there forever. We can't stay out here forever.'

'You think you're gonna—'

'We work out a compromise. There's no other way.'

'You can do that?' There was deep suspicion in the question.

'As long as neither of us make impossible demands.'

'I want out.'

'Of course that's what you want.'

'That, or nothing.'

'We'll talk about it. That, for a beginning.'

'I want more than talk, man.'

'Of course. But first we talk.'

'What do we talk about, copper?'

'My name's Gowan. Chief Superintendent Gowan.'

'So?'

'I think we should exchange names.'

122

'You ain't gonna—'

'Then we shall each know who we're talking to.'

'I ain't no Previous Cons.'

'Have I even suggested—'

'Don't you think that, Gowan.'

'Either way, it's not important.'

'You think I'm green?'

'No.' Gowan paused, then added, 'Not *green*.'

'Okay! Okay!' There was a hard touchiness in the tone. 'I ain't no whitey. So what?'

'Nothing.'

'You ain't gonna—'

'I didn't mean to offend.'

'I'm as English as you are, Gowan.'

'I'm quite sure.'

'That's me, man.'

'I wouldn't deny that.'

'Liverpool, see?'

'Uh-huh.'

'You can't get more English than that.'

'You can't,' agreed Gowan. 'Indeed, I know many Liverpudlians whose speech is not as clear as yours.'

'That's 'cos I'm English, see?'

'Very English.'

'Yeah.'

'So why won't you tell me your name?'

'It's an English name.'

'Of course.'

'A bloody sight more English than *your* name.'

'Gowan is a Gaelic name, I'm afraid.'

'Wallace ain't.'

'No.'

'Wallace is English.'

'A remarkably English name,' said Gowan gently.

'Henry Wallace.'

'Nice.'

'You ain't gonna get any name more English than that, man.'

'Quite so. Now, can we discuss the matter of you leaving the bungalow?'

'My terms, copper.'

'As many of your terms as we can agree upon.'

'Hey! No screwing around with no agreements.'

'You're a sensible man, Wallace. You must be—'

'My terms, or I come out blasting, see?'

'I don't know your terms yet.'

'I just walk out of here, right?'

'Not quite that easy, Henry.'

'You gonna—'

'Not *quite* that easy.'

'You hear me, copper?'

'I have to justify my existence.'

'Eh?'

'I'd be out of a job tomorrow.'

'Who cares?'

'I care.'

'Hey, man, you're gonna—'

'I'm going to talk.' There was the barest hint of firmness in Gowan's tone. 'We're going to talk. That, before either of us makes any threats or any promises.'

'You think I'm gonna—'

'Before either of us agrees to anything. We're going to talk, because the final decision is not up to only me.'

'Eh?'

'It also concerns the Constable you attacked and the Police Sergeant you attacked.'

'Eh?'

'They have some say in what happens next.'

There was a silence which lasted fractionally too long to be a natural pause in the conversation.

Then Wallace said, 'Hey, copper. You trying some sly, smart-arsed trick?'

124

'Why should I?'

'You gonna—'

'I'm going to confer with Constable Walker and Sergeant Blythe. Thanks to what you've done to them, they at least deserve that. When Walker comes out of the operating theatre, when he's fit to discuss things rationally, I'll know exactly how he feels about things. Meanwhile, I'm going to ring off.'

'Hey, copper, I ain't gonna—'

'You're going to think things over, Henry Wallace. You're going to sit down, quieten down and reach certain conclusions. Serious, very serious conclusions. About what you intend doing. About what you seriously expect us to do.'

'Look, man—'

'This is not a motion picture, Henry. This is not a cheap television drama. This is for real. The boat has already sunk, old friend, and unless you make some sort of attempt to swim, you'll go down with it.' There was a pause but Wallace made no attempt to answer. Gowan continued, 'Nobody will interfere; nobody will interrupt you. You have my word on that. You can relax. Relax, weigh the pros against the cons and, when I ring back at noon, we shall, I hope, have some common ground. Be a little nearer to solving what is, at the moment, a difference of opinion.'

'Hey, Gowan, I wanna know what all that crap about—'

'I'll speak to you at twelve, Henry.'

Gowan dropped the receiver onto its rest, then took a deep breath. There was a slight sheen of perspiration on his upper lip and his forehead. Nevertheless, he smiled and murmured, 'Not bad, Constable, for the initial contact, not bad at all.'

Before Tidy could answer, Fuller rounded the corner of the bungalow, saw Gowan's hand still resting on the receiver and exploded pent-up anger.

125

'What in hell's name are you up to, old man! Who the hell gave you permission to shove your personal bloody oar into this particular situation? Damn and blast, haven't I enough worries wet-nursing *real* gold-braided bastards without having to keep an eye on those who should be in wheelchairs?'

## 0945 Hours

For the rest of her life, the sight of a grey-blue Ventolin inhaler would remind Woman Police Sergeant Grant of a good-looking woman apparently fighting for her life; dragging air into her lungs in great, rasping gulps, with her eyes wide and her mouth open. The manageress had opened the ground-floor bedroom window to let in more air, but Blythe's wife, unable to speak, had shaken her head, dragged more air into her lungs and forced it out again. Then, apparently making a supreme effort, she had raised the inhaler to her mouth, closed her lips around the mouthpiece and actuated the aerosol which pushed the salbutamol into her lungs.

Grant, her companion Constable Yates, and the manageress had stood by, helpless and worried. They'd been almost certain that the shock had been too much for the asthmatic, then, gradually, they'd realised that the disease *could* be pushed aside and the breathing brought under some sort of control. It had taken about five minutes before the asthmatic woman had leaned with her back against the bedroom's wardrobe, then nodded before gasping, 'That's it. It's over for the time being. Now tell me again, please.'

That little lot had been easy. Moderately easy. The business of telling a police wife that her husband had been injured, even seriously injured, was nothing when compared with telling a police wife that her husband

126

had been killed; that he'd been murdered. The comparison was like that inflicted by a tennis ball and a cannonball, and the next one out of the barrel was going to be the cannonball!

Police Constable Yates risked a quick glance from the driving seat, saw the look of worried concern on the face of his companion, and said, 'It was very nasty back there for a few minutes.'

'It's always nasty.'

'Aye.'

'And asthma's the very cow of an ailment.'

Yates grunted his agreement.

Grant said, 'I wonder what the hell Walker's wife will be like. What she'll have. A dicky heart, maybe. That's all we need.'

Stan Carter was a one-time copper. Not an ex-copper; not in the usual and normally understood meaning of that expression. He'd *been* in one of the Midland forces for a little more than a year. After that year, he'd had enough. He'd resigned and thereafter he'd horsed around the country trying out a succession of non-skilled and semi-skilled jobs in factories, in local government offices and, when nothing better was on offer, on building sites. He'd even tried self-employment as a jobbing gardener for a spell, but once his name and reputation had become known he'd been rarely offered work.

In sheer desperation he'd tried the police service again, this time as a civilian clerk. He'd landed the job by the skin of his teeth, but of course Carter hadn't known that. And by this time he'd convinced himself that the whole of the police service had been waiting with open arms and baited breath, hoping he'd give them one more chance.

In short, Carter had honed self-kidology into a

127

personal fine art.

He eyed Barstow with pompous disapproval and said, 'All right. We've decided to bail you.'

The manner in which he mouthed the pronoun suggested that he and the Lord Chief Justice of England had retired to discuss the matter, and that only the arguments put forward by Carter himself had swung things in Barstow's favour.

Barstow nodded his thanks.

'I'm bailing you to the local Magistrates' Court. One week on Wednesday. Understood?'

'Yes.'

'On recognisance of fifty pounds. Agreed?'

'Yes.'

Carter handed Barstow a cheap ballpoint and said, 'Usual signature on the Bail Form. And another signature for the return of your property.'

'Thanks.'

As Barstow scrawled his signature, Carter sneered, 'A pity we can't arrange job lots, as far as you're concerned.'

'Without me and people like me you'd be out of a job.' Barstow handed back the ballpoint and began to put loose change, a comb, a wallet and all the bits and pieces that had been taken from him back into various pockets. He said, 'Don't knock us too hard, Mr Carter. It's our weaknesses that puts butter on your bread and sugar into your tea. We make people like you necessary.'

Fuller had been out of order, and Tidy hadn't been too gentle in reminding him of the fact.

He'd said, 'Wind in your horns, Inspector.'

'Eh?' Fuller had stared. Glared.

'Wherever you've been this chap's been carrying *your* corn, and doing it well.' Tidy had flipped a tiny gesture in the direction of Gowan, and added, 'He's been keeping laddo in the bungalow occupied. Doing the job we should have been doing.'

'And who the hell gave him permission to—'

'I did.'

'*You* did? And where the hell did you—'

'Who else?' They'd both moved over the top and were almost bawling at each other. Tidy had snarled, 'You'd disappeared down some rabbit hole. Crosby's been doing his favourite "invisible man" act. Wragg's decided he isn't needed here. If not me, who else?'

'Where the deuce is Wragg?'

'Inspector Fuller, quite frankly I don't give a toss where Wragg is. Or Crosby. Or you. Or anybody! I've been here, up to the eyeballs in blood and shit, too long to care much about *anything*. I was called in to help Blythe, pending the arrival of senior rank. So far you're the only "senior rank" to show, and *you* were only here long enough to show your face before belting off to upset the Headquarters crowd.'

In a quiet, calming voice Gowan said, 'His name is Henry Wallace. He's from Liverpool.'

Fuller's mouth was already open, ready to slang back at Tidy. Instead he closed his mouth, looked at the older man and said, 'Oh!'

'He's frightened,' added Gowan. 'He pretends not to be, but he is.'

'Ah!'

'I think I've convinced him he hasn't yet committed murder. I've told him that the constable is undergoing an operation, but hinted – more than hinted – that he's still alive.'

Fuller blew out his cheeks, then gave a single nod of understanding.

'On the other hand, he's talking about "blasting his way out", whatever that may mean.'

'There are guns in there,' said Fuller flatly.

129

'I gathered that.'

'And thanks to a lunatic decision of the ACC, we can't have guns out here.'

'Guns,' said Gowan gently, 'can sometimes be a very mixed blessing.'

'Yeah.' A slow, shamefaced smile softened Fuller's face, and he said, 'Sorry, Superintendent, I shot my mouth off without giving it too much thought.'

'Don't we all?'

'Anyway, sorry.' Fuller turned to Tidy and added, 'You too, Jim. You've handled things well.'

Tidy grunted a gruff acceptance of the apology.

With far less grace Fuller said, 'Crosby and Wragg, though. Where the hell are *they*?'

Not far from where the exchange between Fuller and Gowan was taking place, various members of the media fraternity were becoming unreasonably impatient. By the nature of things they were anxious for something newsworthy to happen. They didn't want anybody hurt – they were sensible enough not to want that – but they craved for something worthy of large headlines.

The sound engineer from the local BBC region popped a stick of chewing gum into his mouth and began to move his jaws with a steady, rhythmical precision. He was thinking. Normally the Sunday stint was a quiet, almost boring affair; but not today. Today he'd been dragged from bed long before the stint was due to start; he'd linked up with the camera team and the OB reporter and they'd been dumped here in Audsley Avenue, and so far sweet FA had happened.

The sound engineer sat on a handy garden wall, chewed his gum, kept a weather eye on his tape recorder on the pavement near his feet, nursed his mike and allowed his thoughts to wander off to the banks of the River Lune where, had he not been lumbered with

130

this Sunday stint, he would have been snoozing and fishing and generally enjoying himself.

'What's happening?'

The sound engineer was jerked from his day-dreams by the stranger standing at his elbow.

'Eh?' The sound engineer blinked a couple of times.

'There.' The stranger nodded in the direction of the bungalow. 'Something seems to have happened.'

'It has,' agreed the sound engineer.

'What?'

'Look, old son, it's not for me to—'

'It's important.' There was cold insistence there and the stranger's eyes matched the tone of his voice. 'I need to know.'

'There's a chap holed up in the bungalow.' The sound engineer shifted the gum from the left to the right side of his mouth without breaking the rhythm of his jaw. 'The law's waiting for him to show himself.'

'Why?'

'Burglars disturbed, I think.'

'And?'

'A couple of coppers cut up. Badly. Could be one's dead. That's what I hear.'

'As bad as that?'

'All these size tens around, it has to be something. But as usual nobody wants to tell a straight tale.'

'Thanks.'

The stranger hurried towards the roped-off area around the bungalow. He was a moderately built man with close-cropped, sandy-coloured hair. He was wearing a royal blue track-suit with a dark red stripe down the sides of the trousers and the sleeves.

Police Constable Howes figured the morgue as being a deal too innovative for its required purpose. It was, when all was said and done, only a fiddling little

131

mortuary, and part of the cottage hospital at Rogate-on-Sands; a place wherein to hide any cock-ups made by the town's medics; in effect, an ante-chamber to the grave.

There wasn't any real need for the tubular-steel-and-leather high chair; or the desk with the built-in strip-lighting; or the carefully positioned microphone linked up to the wall-mounted cassette recorder.

No wonder the NHS was going down the tube. All this unnecessary gummage for stiffs. Hell alone knew what they got up to with the living.

The door of the morgue opened and the mortuary attendant entered.

'Has he come yet?' he asked.

'Ah, yes. That is, no,' gabbled Howes. 'No. He hasn't arrived yet.'

'You're lucky,' observed the attendant.

'Eh?'

'He has a PM on one of the patients this morning. He's agreed to open up the copper while he's here.'

'To open up the copper'. Howes frowned his silent dislike of the phrase. The attendant was talking about Johnny Walker, a man Howes had always respected; a man who, this very morning – less than four hours back – had paraded for duty with the rest of the shift.

The attendant said, 'We'd better get him stripped off, then.'

'What?'

'The copper. Get him stripped and ready for the slab.'

'Er . . . ' Howes moistened his lips.

'Yes?' The attendant looked puzzled.

'He was a friend of mine, that's all.'

'He isn't now.' The attendant moved towards what looked like a giant filing cabinet with huge drawers. 'Right now he's a friend of nobody's. Eh?'

132

It was meant to be something of a joke, a taste of modern gallows humour, and the attendant grinned.

The attendant hauled at the handle of one of the drawers and it slid out on oiled bearings. The body of Walker was there, under a sheet, and when the attendant pulled the sheet aside Howes saw that his dead colleague's shoes, tunic and trousers had been removed, presumably to get the heavier material away before the blood stiffened too much. But the shirt was soaked, and no doubt the underclothes were, too.

'Up him onto the table.' The attendant bent to take hold of the legs. 'We'd better get him down to the buff before the slasher arrives.'

On the stainless steel table the attendant cut away the rest of Walker's clothes with a pair of large scissors. It was done quickly and expertly, and Howes watched with a faint frown etched across his brow. The damned attendant seemed to be actually enjoying himself; seemed to be getting some sort of morbid pleasure from slicing the cloth, then easing the corpse this way and that in order to ease the material loose.

'They enter the world mother-naked,' observed the attendant. 'They leave the same way, more or less.'

'Eh? Oh yes, I suppose.'

Howes figured the attendant as a definite kink. A real, top-shelf gooley-bird. He obviously handled cadavers with the enthusiasm of a butcher handling a side of prime beef. He tended to slap and punch the corpse, as if sharing a grisly joke with the dead man.

Howes muttered, 'Hey, y'know . . .'

'What's that?'

'I mean, that's Johnny Walker you're handling.'

'Eh?'

'Police Constable Walker.'

'*Was*,' corrected the assistant cheerfully. 'Not any more. Not since he cut himself shaving.'

'That's it!' Howes raised his voice to a near-shouting pitch. 'That's as far as—'

'What's wrong?' The assistant stared. 'I don't know the man. I never met him. Why should I—'

'Shut it!' snarled Howes.

'Hey, I've got a job to do. That's all. I do it. I don't stay awake at nights. I don't—'

'*That!*' Howes pointed at the gaping mouth of the wound at Walker's neck. 'Some – some bastard did *that* to him. And you – you—'

'Not me. Why should I—'

'Respect,' choked Howes, 'for the dead. Some reverence. I'm Coroner's Officer, see? Now – at the moment – that's what I am. And don't you touch him any more. Don't you *touch* him. He's – he *was* my friend. Not to be joked about. Not by you. Not by *anybody*.'


## 1000 Hours

Daniels and Palfrey walked side by side along the promenade. Their speed of walk was little more than a slow, leisurely stroll and to a stranger they might have looked like two holiday-makers making the most of a glorious morning. They each wore lightweight jackets and open-necked shirts. But their talk was not the talk of holiday-makers. Their talk concerned marital love and infidelity.

'I don't think she can help herself.' Daniels' voice was low-pitched and sad. 'I think she tries to be a good wife. I think she really tries.'

Palfrey seemed to have difficulty in voicing his views. He had a tendency to moisten his lips between each sentence.

He said, 'What about the marriage guidance people?'

'I'm a copper.'

134

'I don't see what that has to do—'

'We're expected to be solid. Respectable. Not given to running to other people with our troubles.'

They continued their slow walk in step, not too far from the promenade railings and with the sun high above their left shoulders.

Palfrey seemed to hesitate, then said, 'It doesn't follow, you know.'

'What?'

'Whatever your occupation, whatever your profession or calling, you sometimes need help. Marriages go wrong for all sorts of reasons.'

'Coppers are expected to set an example.'

'So are parsons,' said Palfrey quietly. Then, 'Sometimes they set a bad example.'

'Anyway . . .' Daniels scowled at the wavelets which were edging the tide across the surface of the sand towards the base of the prom. His tone was contemptuous when he continued. 'Marriage guidance? It's staffed with do-gooders. Half of 'em don't even know.'

'Know?'

'The stresses. The strains. What can really go wrong in a marriage. It's all book-learning.'

'Oh, I wouldn't say that.'

'I would.'

'They're trained men and women. Very intelligent. Very understanding.'

'Would you?' demanded Daniels.

'What?'

'Suppose your marriage was a bit rocky, would you open your heart to complete strangers? Would you tell 'em all the ins and outs?'

Palfrey took a deep breath and said, 'You're telling me.'

'That's different.'

'Surely not.'

135

'You're a clergyman. The parish priest. You're different.'

'I wish . . .' sighed Palfrey, then closed his mouth before ending the sentence.

They walked in silence for about twenty yards. They reached the pier head and Palfrey stopped, hesitantly.

Daniels, too, came to a halt. He said, 'I'll make my way home.' In a voice that carried a small sigh, he added, 'Kiss and make up. That's what it boils down to, every time.'

Daisy was normally a quiet little donkey; sweet-tempered and happy to carry children, from tots to teenagers, back and forth across the stretch of sand which, in effect, was the 'beat' of herself and her half-dozen stable-mates. She didn't mind. Even when the youth whose job it was to keep an eye on things ran behind, waving a stick and shouting, she didn't mind. It was all make-believe. She continued to trot along at her own speed, not a stride faster and not a yard farther before she turned for the return trot, but everybody was happy and none more happy than Daisy.

But now she was not happy.

Somebody had left the gate of the paddock ajar and, being of an inquisitive turn of mind, she'd ventured into the outside world alone. She'd made her way towards the shore. She'd discovered the municipal flower bed, and she'd rather enjoyed the taste of the flowers. In the event she'd eaten too much, a lot too much, and now she had an annoying belly-ache. She wished she was back in the paddock with her buddies.

Constable Vine, of course, did not know all these things. What is more, being Constable Vine, he would not have believed that a mere donkey could be subjected to such moods and disappointments. As far as Vine was concerned, Daisy was only a common-or-

136

garden moke and one more irritation to be suffered on this Sunday early shift.

Which is why when Vine entered the dog pound he, for no good reason, gave Daisy a sharp smack across the rump with his open palm.

Which, in turn, is why Daisy reacted. She kicked. Twice. Her tiny rear hooves lashed outward and upwards in a swift, twinkling wham-wham. And each time the kick found a mark.

Her left hoof caught Vine under the kneecap. As he doubled in pain, her right hoof landed full in Vine's descending face. Specifically, on the bridge of his nose.

Vine screamed with sudden agony. His eyes overflowed with tears and his nose gushed scarlet. He staggered from the dog pound and, holding his face, limped towards the rear door of the Rogate-on-Sands Police Station.

Fuller waved a dismissal to the uniformed constable who'd tried to keep the blue-track-suited man away from the bungalow, and asked, 'Sergeant? Royal Marines?'

'Yes.'

'You have means of identity, of course?'

'If necessary, but not with me.' The man's eyes fixed themselves on Fuller's face as he continued, 'I have good reason to believe my aunt is in this bungalow.'

'Your aunt?' Fuller was worried about making too many mistakes. His progress towards a decision was painfully slow.

'Agnes Littlewood.'

'You think she's in there?'

'She left for this address early this morning. She hasn't yet arrived home.'

'Why did she come here?'

'She cleans for Arkwright. Keeps an eye on the place

137

when he's away, and at the moment he's on holiday.'

'Your aunt?' repeated Fuller.

The man said, 'I'm due back at base by midnight tomorrow. If anything's happened, I'd better try for an extension.'

'Should something have happened?' teased Fuller. 'Might something have happened?'

'Can we talk?' asked the man tightly.

'We *are* talking, surely.'

'Privately?'

Fuller nodded and led the way to the garden hut which stood alongside the greenhouse. The man closed the door, but still hesitated before he spoke.

Then he murmured, 'SBS.'

'I beg your pardon?'

'The Special Boat Squadron. I'm attached.'

'Oh!'

'Now, can we please stop pussyfooting around and get a straight answer to a straight question. What's happening here?'

'From what I gather,' Fuller was still a little wary, 'so far, nobody's been able to give a clear, unvarnished yarn. There was a break-in. A coloured youth, from Liverpool. He was disturbed by a patrolling constable. He killed the constable; he opened his throat with a cut-throat razor. Then, when a uniformed sergeant tried to move the body, he did an encore with the razor and opened the sergeant's face and arm.'

'And he's still in there? The coloured youth?'

'He's still in there,' said Fuller grimly. 'And his next port of call is a police cell.'

'And my aunt?'

'It's possible.' Fuller chose his words with care. 'She was seen going in. Nobody's mentioned seeing her leave.'

'She could be dead?' The SBS man's voice was low

138

and calm but very cold.

'We have no means of knowing.'

'She could be dead?'

'I'm not prepared to—'

'Hell's teeth, man. If he's killed one and maimed another. If she's still in there, she could be dead.'

'It's a possibility we must accept.' The words sounded pompous, and Fuller knew that. In a more relaxed tone he added, 'I hope not. The bastard's done too much already.'

'Other than the razor—' began the SBS man.

'We don't know.' Fuller fielded the question before it had fully arrived. 'I'm told the man, Arkwright, was something of a gun nut. There's been wild talk about him "blasting his way out". I'm sorry. You want the truth? By any yardstick, the situation isn't too healthy.'

The SBS man moved his head in a single, slow nod, then said, 'I'm staying.'

'Look, I don't know—'

'It's *my* aunt in there. I want to know, and as soon as possible. I want to know how to act.'

'What, exactly, does that mean?'

'If she is dead; if he has killed her—'

'Whatever.' Fuller put bite into his tone. 'It's our job. We handle it our way. No cowboy-and-Indian tactics.'

'She's family.' The SBS man's voice was low-pitched and soft. 'She's the only family I've got. I'm the only family she's got. I'm making no promises.'

'Sergeant, I'll not be hampered by—'

'And I'm staying. Whatever rank you carry, it doesn't intimidate me.'

It was a well-built semi of Accrington brick with a tiny, neatly hedged front garden, a not-quite-as-neat rear garden and a wide path down the side of the house upon which to park the Ford Fiesta that had once been

139

the pride of Constable Walker's life. The furniture was sufficient, without it adding up to clutter; there was a Welsh dresser, a TV set, a music centre, a bookcase stacked with club-bound books, two armchairs and a sofa. The carpet was fitted and the rug in front of the electric fire tried hard to give the impression of genuine Indian.

It was, in the opinion of Woman Police Sergeant Grant, a nice, comfortable, come-day-go-day, find-one-at-every-street-corner house.

On the other hand (and, again, in the opinion of WPS Grant) the woman was quite unique.

A wide-eyed Grant almost gasped, 'You do understand what I've just told you? Why we're here?'

'Of course. Walker's dead.'

She was a dumpy woman with greying hair. She wore a jazzy, floral shirt outside loose-fitting trousers. She'd been dead-heading flowers when they'd arrived and, other than kicking off what were obviously 'gardening shoes', she'd obediently led them into the house and into the front room before lowering herself into one of the armchairs. She'd taken the news without a hint of emotion.

'Your husband,' said Grant. Then, 'I'm sorry, but—' and then she closed her mouth, because she was at a loss for words.

'My husband's dead.' She allowed herself a quick, tight-lipped smile. Then she said, 'Your name is Grant, isn't it?'

'Yes.'

'You're not married, of course.'

'No, but—'

'If you were married, you might understand.'

Grant slowly sat down on the twin armchair. She seemed to be in deeper shock than the woman who'd just been widowed. Police Constable Yates stood by the closed door of the front room, blinked occasionally,

140

kept a deadpan expression on his face and said nothing.

Grant said, 'This is new to me.'

'New?' Walker's widow sounded politely interested.

'This situation. Your reaction is not what we're expected to—'

'You mean honesty?'

'Honesty? Or are you trying to shock?'

'Honesty – genuine honesty – sometimes does shock. Didn't you know?'

'Johnny Walker was a—'

'John Walker was a prolonged pain in the rump. I should know. I lived with him.'

Grant opened her mouth to speak, then thought better of it and closed her mouth again.

Walker's widow said, 'A personal opinion, of course. But marriages, all marriages, should have a statutory time limit attached. Five years. No more than seven. After that they become boring, Miss Grant. Unutterably and monumentally boring. Boredom gradually turns to dislike. Dislike to hatred. But all the time there's this unnecessary make-believe crap. All this happy-ever-after bull. But it's not so. It never is so.' She paused, swallowed and then, in a voice which carried the hint of a croak, went on, 'That's the con. That's where the heartache comes. That it never can be. That the "forever" promise is a big fat lie. After the first few years, you start scratching at each other. Then it's all the time. You look for faults. Look for reasons or excuses to argue. There's no love left. Not even respect. *Nothing!* You can't even see each other without hurting each other. You don't really need a reason. You just want to hurt. All day. Every day.'

It was a little like a dam, starting to crack under impossible pressure. First a hairline fracture, then a gradual widening; finally there would be an explosion and a complete destruction.

141

Grant and Yates watched wide-eyed as the woman continued her terrifying self-annihilation.

'It's not how they tell it in books, is it? Not like that, at all. Not love. Not even liking. You know each other too well. Inside out. Back to front. Every weakness. Every fault. And that's all you can see. All the time. The bad things. The hateful things you'd never noticed before. That's all you can see.'

She paused to lick the moisture from her lips, and the moisture came from the streams of tears which spilled from her eyes. But she seemed to be completely unaware that she was crying, and even when her heartbreak threatened to choke her she continued trying to speak. Harsh words, which were meaningless in a voice that was cracked and hoarse.

'That's what you live on, mutual hatred. Not love. Not even friendship. Kind words? What are kind words? After so long, you never give them. Never receive them. It's all twisted up. What you had, or once had, or *thought* you once had ... it's gone. Dead. You can never ... never ...'

She seemed to cave-in upon herself; as if she'd suddenly become hollow, an empty shell incapable of even retaining its shape. And the tears came flooding out. And the shoulder-shaking sobs. And the fighting to force words out that wouldn't make their way past her throat.

Grant pushed herself forward and out of the armchair. She knelt beside the weeping woman, put her arm around her shoulder and cooed, 'It's all right, my lovely. Let it come. We understand. We'll stay. However long you need us, we'll stay.'

## 1015 Hours

Constable Wood figured himself as Jack-the-Lad. And why not? He'd run his Divisional Superintendent ragged. More than that, even. The fall of the dice had resulted in Crosby kissing a lamp standard with his fancy car and, as a result, ending up with a severe headache and, possibly, a Notice of Intended Prosecution for a Road Traffic Offence.

Wood had ambled quietly back to his home territory of C Beat. He'd called in for a fag and a chat at a small, off-the-coast guest house whose proprietor was an ex-jockey who occasionally passed on information about 'sure things'. Then he went on to a market-garden emporium, where he'd munched a tomato plucked straight from its plant, discussed the possibility of picking up cheap mushroom compost and agreed to do a few hours 'moonlighting', mowing lawns for customers next week. And now he was making his way towards a quick-snack café, where he usually enjoyed a buckshee, mid-morning sandwich when he was on the early shift.

Which was when Constable Wood's personal dreamboat hit rough water.

The man who rounded the corner about fifty yards in front of Wood was travelling at a neat lick. He was heel-toeing it, in true walking-race expertise. His elbows were tucked into his sides and brushing his ribs as his forearms pumped away like pistons, in time with the stiff-legged, rolling gait. The man was in his late-to-mid-sixties – maybe even past the seventy mark – white-haired and thin, obviously very fit and quite naked.

He seemed to be completely unimpressed by the open-mouthed stares of the passing pedestrians. His

143

head was down, his hair was swinging in time with his body rhythm and he was obviously enjoying himself.

Wood blinked his amazement, then deliberately blocked the walker's path. He allowed him to collide head-on, and as the older man staggered back and regained his balance, Wood said, 'Take it easy, old man. You seem to have come out without your pants.'

'What?' The walker waved a hand, as if to brush aside this annoying inconvenience. 'I have at least another three miles to go before the finishing tape.'

'Old man,' Wood put out a restraining hand, 'in that state, you'll startle the horses. Be a good chap and—'

'Make way, you young whippersnapper.' The walker moved forward as if to bore a way through Wood. He did more than that, even. He lowered a clenched fist and drove it hard into Wood's testicles as he snapped, 'Move, you disgusting little creature. Make way for your betters.'

'I'll – I'll—' Wood gasped for breath as he doubled in pain. Then, as the elderly walker tried to pass, he grabbed a wiry upper arm and held on.

There was an uncommon amount of pulling and pushing; had not Wood been in some agony, or had the elderly walker been wearing clothes, there might have been an element of farce in the incident. The onlookers watched with open interest as they wrestled and as, eventually, Wood forced an arm-lock on the struggling oldster and pointed him in the direction of Rogate-on-Sands Police Station.

If the pathologist hadn't been a man of understanding, Howe's might have had some difficulty in arguing his case. Her Majesty's Coroner had been notified of the Sudden Death of Police Constable Walker, if, by 'notification' you mean that HM Coroner *knew* about it. He'd been telephoned and he, in turn, had

144

telephoned the pathologist and had arranged for the normal post-mortem examination. That much was true. It was also true that the force (like so many provincial forces) didn't run to a single Coroner's Officer; that the copper lumbered with the Sudden Death automatically took on the authority of the Coroner's representative.

When, therefore, Howes claimed to be Coroner's Officer, he truly believed he was stating no less than the truth.

But of course the official written notification had yet to take place. That was the weakness of Howes' argument; that HM Coroner wasn't yet aware of the officer who was his present Officer. And an awkward pathologist might have turned nasty.

As it was, when Howes had motioned towards the mortuary assistant and said, 'I don't want *him* present at the post-mortem,' the pathologist had looked a little surprised, and had then nodded and said, 'You're the Coroner's Officer,' and it had been as simple as that.

The mortuary assistant had looked a little crestfallen but had had no real choice. In fairness, Howes was helping with the autopsy as much as he was able.

'Your friend?' The pathologist had opened up the body and was examining the gullet with gloved fingers.

'I – er – liked him,' stumbled Howes.

'The usual man – the man you've just dismissed – has grown a little insensitive over the years.'

'Yes, I suppose that's it.'

'A nasty wound. A very sharp knife.'

'A cut-throat, y'know, an open razor, I think.'

'That would do the trick.' The pathologist placed the gullet, windpipe and lungs on the slab alongside the body. As he removed the kidneys from the cavity he murmured, 'Signs of renal calculi. The man must have lived with some degree of pain.'

'Oh!'

145

'He never complained?'

'I wouldn't know.'

As he continued the various stages of the autopsy, the pathologist talked. Possibly to himself, although Howes thought it only polite to acknowledge periodically what was being said. Yet it was not really a conversation, more an airing of views interspersed with noises of agreement.

'A strange animal, the homo sapiens. Expert opinion suggests he's the only animal capable of appreciating his own end, and the knowledge scares him silly. Pain, for example. He's scared of pain, so he pretends it isn't there. Takes analgesics to deaden the pain. But pain doesn't kill; pain is only a symptom. It's a warning that something's wrong. Remove the pain and who knows? It's like removing a red danger signal. Y'know something? Something people like me become very aware of?'

The pathologist poked at the intestines with gloved fingers and, not for the first time, Howes was amazed at the amount of offal tucked away in the lower part of a human trunk.

The pathologist continued, 'Get to be forty or thereabouts, and that's when you know you're not immortal. Kids, teenagers and young people, to them death is a very abstract thing. It doesn't apply. They're going to live forever. Until they're about forty or thereabouts, then they get scared. Really scared, when they can bring themselves round to thinking about it.'

'Yeah, I suppose so.'

'That's when a lot of 'em start going to church.'

'Oh!'

'It's a sort of long-stop. They go often, to try to make up for lost time. They're "born again". That's what they call themselves.'

'Does that mean . . .' Howes hesitated.

'What?'

'That you don't believe? You're not religious?'

146

'This.' The pathologist brought a gloved palm down on the dead man's thigh. It made a crack rather than a slap, and the difference made Howes blink. The pathologist continued, 'This isn't – what's his name?'

'Walker. Johnny Walker.'

'This isn't your friend, Walker. Not this. We can make this. Mary Shelley wasn't so very outrageously frightening, Constable. When she thought up the monster, it couldn't be done. But today it's no real problem. We could construct it. Easily. In effect, a bit at a time, it happens every day in a hundred operating theatres. The bits and pieces. The things you can see. The things you can handle. But not the important, the invisible bits. The brain, sure, but not the mind. We don't know what "thought" is. We know it's there, but that's all we do know. The body, but not the *soul*. Not *life*. That's beyond us. As a personal opinion, it always will be. It's where faith takes over. Where religion starts.'

The pathologist re-located the bits and pieces in the stomach cavity as he continued.

'Christianity, it's a strange religion. We call our God-head by his first name. Ever thought about that? The Islam boys don't call him "Charlie" Mohammed. It's not "Fred" Buddha. But it's *Jesus* Christ. It makes you wonder. It makes *me* wonder. Who the hell do we think we are?'

As piers go, Rogate-on-Sands pier was nothing to write home about. It had a pin-table hall at the entrance; a place with blacked-out windows, flashing lights, laser illuminations; a typical grotto geared to take the coins from suckers. Thereafter it was a planked walkway, barely ten yards wide and little more than fifty yards long. Supreme optimists tossed weighted lines into the waves when the tide was in, and hoped some dab might fancy the bait. There was a small, weather-battered café

147

at the pier end and, along the centre of the walkway, long, back-to-back benches allowed those who didn't mind the discomfort to sit and look up and down the coast. There was even a so-called pavilion, originally built to house concert parties and the like, then used as the town's disco, but these days used as a store-room for oak planks, barrels of paint, sacks of screws and nails and all the other remarkably diverse requirements for keeping even a modest pier under constant repair and able to withstand the buffeting of the weather.

The Reverend Reginald Palfrey sat on one of the benches in the centre of the pier and watched the tide through the narrow crack between the planks of the walkway. The waves swirled and sloshed around the iron uprights of the pier as the water crept slowly towards the base of the promenade. To watch the swing and whirl of the sea through the gap was almost hypnotic and the man had to speak twice before Palfrey became aware of his presence.

Then the clergyman looked up, blinked away the hint of dizziness and said, 'Oh! Ah, yes. Barstow. What a surprise, what a pleasant surprise. I rather expected you to be among the congregation at this time on a Sunday morning.'

'Yes.' Barstow gave a quick, timid smile. 'And I would have expected you to be in front of the congregation.' Then, in a quick, apologetic tone, 'Are you ill? Is that it? Is that why—'

'Sit down, Mr Barstow.' Palfrey patted the bench seat. 'Please. Unless you haven't time, I'd like to talk. To somebody. To you. Please.'

'And where the steaming hell have you been?' Fuller spotted Detective Sergeant Wragg trying to nip through the gate of the bungalow without being noticed. He snarled, 'We all thought you'd opted for early retirement. We were thinking of organising a whip-round for a going-away present.'

Wragg was conscious of the uniformed officers within hearing distance, all trying to make-believe they couldn't hear Fuller's angry sarcasm. He muttered, 'The various points around the bungalow; I've been checking them.'

'Checking them?'

'That they're all covered. That he can't—'

'You've been nowhere near the bloody bungalow,' raged Fuller. 'You've been skiving off somewhere. Just because we won't buy your own brand of death-or-glory tactics you opted out of the incident and went to walk off your sulks.'

'I've been to the hospital. I've—'

'I could have *built* a bloody hospital by this time.'

Gowan moved in and touched Fuller's arm. In a soothing tone he said, 'Inspector.' He glanced towards the bungalow. 'Don't play into his hands.'

'Eh?'

'A cool head, that's what we all need. Don't let things ruffle you.'

'I'm damned if I'm going to —'

'You'll regret it,' warned Gowan. 'Later, when this is over, roast him by all means, but for the moment forget it. You have some very important decisions to make. Don't let—'

Fuller interrupted what Gowan was saying by yelling, '*Down!*' and at the same time grabbing the older man by the shoulders and literally throwing him onto the soil beside the path.

Gowan had been standing with his back to the bungalow. Fuller, on the other hand, had been almost facing the rear door and had seen the door being yanked open and the coloured hooligan, Wallace, standing at the threshold holding a double-barrelled shotgun.

As the two men hit the soil the first barrel spouted

149

flame and shot and the creosoted fence in front of which they'd been standing showed pockmarks and splinters.

That was when Wragg lost control. As Fuller and Gowan hit the ground he sprinted forward, across the path and at an angle to the rear door of the bungalow. He was trying for a zig-zag approach, in order to make aiming more difficult for the gunman. It was a mad thing to do but it also had a touch of sheer magnificence.

Because he was watching Wragg, and trying to line up the shotgun on the racing detective, Wallace didn't see the Special Boat Squadron sergeant also move into action. The SBS man sensed what was going to happen, hared across the grass, then hurled himself in a horizontal rugby tackle at Wragg's waist. They came down in a rolling bundle as the twelve-bore exploded for a second time and one of the pellets nicked Wragg's forehead above the right eye and dropped a thin ribbon of blood towards the eyebrow.

The two sergeants scrambled to their feet and raced for the coloured gunman. The gunman panicked, spun on his heels and ducked back into the bungalow. He slammed the door closed and the Yale lock clicked into place a shaved second before the sergeants hit the door panels.

Panting, they each ended with their back pressed against the brickwork at the side of the locked door, one on the left and one on the right. As they regained their breath a double-blast came from inside the bungalow and a jagged, splinter-edged hole the size of a dinner plate appeared in the middle of the door just below chest level.

Away from the door, Gowan was pushing himself upright.

He said, 'Well, at least now we know. He does have a

150

gun, and ammunition.'

As he spoke he glanced at Fuller, and what he saw brought a worried expression to his face.

Fuller was on all fours, his head hung low between his stiffened arms. He was making tiny mewing noises and moving his head in slow pendulum movements from side to side.

'Inspector.' Gowan's voice was soft, but urgent. When Fuller didn't answer, he said, 'Inspector, are you all right?'

Fuller raised his head, but stayed down on all fours. His face was creased and ugly with a torment he couldn't control.

He whimpered, 'He'll kill somebody.'

'Not if we—'

'He'll kill somebody. And *I* can't stop him. They won't listen, and I don't carry the rank. He'll kill somebody, and they'll all blame me.'

'Don't arrest him.' The man was remarkably neat, with a trimmed beard, a short-back-and-sides haircut and a white, open-necked, short-sleeved shirt. He said, 'I know him. Periodically he's a resident at The Willows. He's harmless. I'll take him home.'

'Harmless?' Constable Wood kept the arm-lock on the elderly nudist and glared his disagreement. 'This silly old buffer just about ripped my balls out by the roots.'

'He didn't mean any harm. He's not quite—'

'Y'mean he hasn't both oars in the water?'

'Look, Constable. I'm a male nurse at The Willows.'

'The nut-house?'

'I hope,' said the neatly dressed man solemnly, 'that you never need the services we provide.' Then, with a touch of impatience, 'No, it's not a nut-house, as you're pleased to call it. We help people to rest and come to terms with situations they can't handle. People like Ted

151

Calverly, here.'

'Is that his name?'

'That's his name.' The neatly dressed man nodded.

A small crowd had gathered and a middle-aged man, more compassionate than the rest, removed his own lightweight jacket and tied it, apron-fashion, around the waist of the elderly man.

The neatly dressed man said, 'He was once rather famous, you know.'

'Who? This old barmpot?'

'In the nineteen-forty-eight London Olympics he was due to represent the United Kingdom. In walking. He slipped and cracked his ankle three days before the opening ceremony.'

Somebody in the tiny crowd said, 'Let him go, Constable. He's done no harm.'

'Has he?' asked the neatly dressed man.

'You know where he lives?' growled Wood.

'I'll call a taxi and take him back to The Willows. We'll notify his son from there.'

The elderly man was blinking his way back to full realisation of where he was and what was happening. He pleaded, 'Look, I'm not too sure . . . I'm sorry, but—'

'That's all right, Mister Calverly.' The neatly dressed man took an elbow and, with some reluctance, Wood slowly released the arm-lock. The neatly dressed man continued, 'We'll have you between cool sheets in no time at all. Just relax. You're with friends. Nobody's going to harm you.'

'Just get him off the street,' warned Wood. 'That's all. Get him off the street and where he can't cause a public nuisance.'

## 1030 Hours

Jim Tidy stayed in the background and watched the retired Hong Kong policeman trying to keep Fuller's temporary crack-up from the media people. It wouldn't do to let the TV, the radio and the newspaper people know that the man nominally in charge of the incident suffered from the ordinary, human weakness of blind, overpowering panic. That our policemen are wonderful was the popular belief of most law-abiding citizens. But our policemen are merely men wearing a particular uniform. And sometimes not even that. Tidy knew the truth of it.

Not too many weeks ago he, Jim Tidy, had buckled and almost broken under the weight of a personal anguish. He'd had verified what he'd already suspected and almost known: that police wives, too, were a vital part of the service. That they were taken for granted until they were no longer there.

But then, when they suddenly *weren't* there . . .

Madge had been a great deal more than a wife. More than a companion, more than a friend, more than a lover. She'd been part of his police service; as much a part of his police service as any of his fellow coppers. She'd been there, a warm and comforting haven of safety and sanity, to which he could scurry when things grew too hairy. When the yobs had chanced their arm, and the odds in favour of being downed or kicked unconscious had seemed to be too heavy for comfort. When the well-heeled lunatics had had too much booze and were prepared to do stupid and irrational things, merely to impress their female counterparts. When it hadn't happened, but when it might easily have happened, and when the copper's nerves had been stretched to within a whisker of breaking-point. Then –

153

when it was over and the snapping point had passed –
the tiny uncontrollable trembling had taken over. Then
Madge had been *there*, to help take the strain and steady
everything back to normality.

Tidy knew. Every copper with any street experience
behind him knew. Hopefully, Gowan knew.

But the media people wouldn't know.

Tidy divided his attention between the door,
alongside which stood Wragg and the man in the blue
track-suit, and Gowan and Fuller. It was one of those
moments. It would pass. They always passed. But until
it passed, it was a little like a slow-burning fuse which,
unless it was extinguished, would eventually reach the
powder keg and explode.

Meanwhile Tidy watched and worried.


Stan Carter ran the palm of his right hand over the
gloss of his bald pate, looked solemnly at the man who'd
arrived at the public counter and said, 'Right. Can I
help you?'

'Somebody's stolen one of my donkeys.' He was a
short-statured man, well-tanned and wrinkled. He had
short-cropped, wavy hair with pronounced sideburns.
His clothes were worn but clean; khaki drill trousers
and a khaki shirt, open-necked and with the sleeves
rolled up above the elbows. He continued, 'Last night I
paddocked them. This morning one's missing and the
gate's been opened.'

Carter put on a superior look and said, 'We have it in
the back.'

'Eh?'

'Your donkey's in the back, in the dog pound. We
found it wandering last night.'

'D'you get the bloke who pinched her?'

'She wasn't stolen.'

'Oh, aye?' The man nodded. 'She was pinched. She's a

154

clever girl, but not clever enough to unlatch that gate.'

Constable Vine wandered into the Front Office from somewhere deep within the depths of the police station. He still held a handkerchief to a red and slightly swollen nose.

Carter said, 'This fellow's come for his donkey.'

'Oh, aye?' Vine's eyes glinted. He lowered the handkerchief and said, 'What's the big idea, then?'

'Eh?' The little man stared.

'Letting the bloody thing wander the streets all night.'

'I didn't.'

'Eating half the flowers in the municipal gardens.'

'Look, I'm not—'

'Among other things, it's a dangerous bloody animal. It should be locked safely away.'

'It *was* locked safely away. It's been pinched. That's why I'm here. Because I want whoever pinched her found and put away.'

'Bloody thing kicked me in the face,' snarled Vine.

'Never!'

'If it's your frigging donkey, it kicked me in the face.'

Carter backed away from the public counter. In order to find something to do, he turned and re-checked the messages in the Telephone Message Book. The exchanges between Vine and the little man were becoming a little too heated for comfort.

'She was pinched,' insisted the little man.

'Don't be daft.'

'I want whoever pinched her put away.'

'Sing-Sing, Colditz or Siberia?' asked Vine sarcastically.

'She's very good with kids. She's very intelligent. I want whoever pinched her—'

'You're out of your mind.' Vine's voice was harsh and impatient. 'If you think I'm going through the whole palaver of Crime Complaint, Crime Report, Christ only

155

knows how many statements, telephoning the details throughout the section and all the rest of it, just because you forgot to shut a bloody gate.'

'I didn't forget to shut the—'

'Take your stupid donkey, and be glad we don't charge you with damage to the plants and flowers it's chewed up.'

The little man tightened his lips. His nostrils quivered as he said, 'Right. I want to see whoever's in charge.'

'Such a simple word. Such a nice word.' Palfrey stared with out-of-focus eyes at the quivering reflection of the sun on the dancing, incoming wavelets. It might have been mistakenly assumed that he was talking to Barstow. Barstow was sitting beside him on the pier bench, listening without interruption. Shocked, perhaps, but successfully hiding all expression of even mild outrage.

Palfrey continued, 'Why did these people choose the word "gay"? It's such an innocent word, so childlike. D'you remember the film, *The Gay Divorce*? Or the show, *Gay's The Word*? Such an ordinary word, in the old days. Before perverts like me filched it.'

Above their heads, the gulls screamed their delight at catching the few thermals available in the hot mid-morning. They sat with outstretched wings on the rising air. Not flying. Swinging, first left then right, in what was to them a natural but magical harnessing of one of nature's invisible forces.

'. . . It meant something more childlike than "happy". It had an air of guileless rusticity. It had ribbons attached. Picnics. Poke-bonnets.'

They were black-faced gulls with their legs tucked tightly behind them. Ill-tempered, squabbling creatures, spoiled by modern civilisation but still wild and suspicious.

156

'. . . Last night, I went up the coast. To Blackpool. To a "Singles Bar" – that's what they call them. I doubt if there are any at Rogate. A Singles Bar favoured by homosexuals, gays and lesbians. They call it love. A love ordinary people don't understand. A pettish, quick-tempered kind of love. Coupled with an irritating arrogance. Bitter. Sharp-edged. Love I can never, ever understand.'

On the road beyond Rock Walk a motorcycle engine kicked into life, a powerful engine with a defective silencer in its exhaust chamber. It sent the echoes growling and rattling from the walls of the sea-front hotels and blocks of flats and apartments, then its pitch rose and, very gradually, it faded away as machine and rider moved south along the coast road.

'. . . Saint Paul doesn't mince words, you know. He condemns what we call "gay love" without qualification. It's wrong. It's unnatural. And people like me shouldn't even try to excuse it, much less practise it.'

Very gently Barstow said, 'Saint Paul never knew Christ.'

Palfrey seemed to blink himself back to the here-and-now. The lost expression eased, and the eyes slowly moved to focus on Barstow's face.

Barstow's voice became stronger and more confident as he continued, 'Paul had a vision, no more than a vision, on the Damascus Road. What he saw, I don't know. Just that it changed him. He turned from a passionate enemy into a passionate believer. But he never walked with Christ; it was all theory. Not like Peter. Peter *knew* Christ, knew him as a friend. A saviour, too, of course, but as a friend. More intimately. More closely than Paul could ever know him.'

Palfrey frowned, as if trying to bring his concentration under tighter control.

He said, 'That's not right, Barstow. That's not how

157

you should—'

'It's what I think,' said Barstow heatedly. 'It's what I've thought for a long time. Paul. As Saul, he was a tyrant. Some sort of minor autocrat. A typical town-hall bully. I've no doubt he took part in minor orgies. They all did, his type; it was part of the way of life. Maybe that's why he changed his name. Paul wasn't Saul. What Saul had done, Paul would never do. Self-deception, you see. It's not something new. It's happened over the centuries. Hypocrites. Men who have said, "Don't do as I do. Do as I say." Or in the case of Paul, "Don't do as I *did*." It's possible. I think it's more than possible.'

Barstow paused, as if shocked by the intensity of his own outburst. Then he jutted his chin a little and continued.

'Peter was different. Peter listened and learned. He knew how to excuse, to forgive. Peter was close to Christ and tried to be like Christ. He was a simple man and didn't try to be special. He knew what fear was, what being weak was. He even denied the Saviour. I don't think he liked Paul. I don't think he quite believed him. It comes out in the Bible, as I see it. It's difficult, our religion. Yours and mine. It's very difficult. But Paul makes it impossible, that's how I see it. Paul asks too much. Christ asks only what you can give.'

The SBS sergeant's name was Littlewood. The same name as his aunt. There was about him that hard, lean and fit bearing which comes from the iron discipline of Special Duties, superimposed upon the natural self-control of a Royal Marine NCO.

He motioned Tidy to come closer and, with the same movement, motioned Wragg to stay in position at the other side of the bungalow's rear door.

In a soft, gentle whisper which carried no farther than Tidy's ear, he said, 'He has an advantage. It's dark

158

in the back entrance. We can't see him, but he can see us.' As Tidy nodded an understanding, he continued, 'We kill that advantage. Keep out of sight from the hole in the door. In the garden shed there'll be, maybe, a sacking, some nails and a hammer. And get that useless bugger out of range.' He nodded towards the still-crouching Fuller. 'And the old man.' As Tidy nodded further understanding, Littlewood ended, 'And if you see something like a sledge-hammer, get it over here.'

Daniels sprawled in an armchair with his chin on his chest, and gazed at the two people with whom his life was intrinsically entangled, his wife and his brother. Decisions had been reached. Cold-blooded, uninhibited decisions which, a few hours previously, would have seemed impossible.

He growled, 'We know where we stand. All three of us.'

Chris and Beth Daniels made soft noises denoting understanding. They made no objections. They didn't argue. They were both content to let Charlie Daniels set his own pace for the future, if only because that was the only future available.

'Beth?' said Daniels.

'Just that it makes me feel like—'

'A whore?' The question ended her sentence for her, and she had the grace to blush. Daniels continued, 'Why not? That's what you are. You're nobody's wife. You don't deserve to be anybody's wife. Chris had you before I had you. He's had you since I had you. We just don't lie anymore. We share you, that's all. But we do it openly.'

Chris Daniels shifted uncomfortably in the twin armchair and muttered, 'Look, Charlie, I don't think you should—'

159

'That's right. You don't think.' Charlie Daniels watched the younger man's face as he spoke. 'Your salad days are finished, little brother. You've had your last free ride on the roundabout. Tomorrow, we visit the solicitor's office. Red Tape and pink ribbon. I want you tied up in it. You're going to be tied up in it, both of you, then *you're* going to work your balls off.'

He stared at his brother and felt no hint of affection, merely that he was the other son of his mother. That was the only link he had with the other man; the love he had had for his mother. There was no love for him as a brother.

'You really dislike me.' There was genuine surprise in Chris Daniels' tone. 'I mean really hate me.'

'Both of you,' agreed Charlie Daniels quietly. 'I'm a slow learner, but given time . . .'

He left the sentence unfinished and suspended in mid-air. There was a silence, a strange, highly charged, awkward silence which, it seemed, Chris and Beth dared not break. The aversion and disgust were almost tangible. There was nothing remissive in Charlie Daniels' expression, or the way he slumped in the armchair and slowly moved his gaze from his brother to his wife then back again.

'We make a great team,' he murmured contemptuously. 'The cuckolded husband, the unfaithful wife and the rammish brother. We should tour the halls. We'd get a big laugh.'

## 1045 Hours

Rogate-on-Sands Cottage Hospital. It was a nice name. A comforting name. And as far as possible, it lived up to its name. Unlike the big hospitals at Blackpool and Preston, at Southport and Liverpool, it was exactly what

160

it sounded, a cottage hospital. Specialists visited on a fairly regular basis. No fancy, spare-part surgery was performed in its two moderately well-equipped theatres. There was no Emergency or Intensive Care Unit. It was not equipped to handle the carnage from an even moderate road traffic shunt-up. Nevertheless, and fortunately for Police Sergeant Joseph Blythe, one of the general surgeons based at the Preston hospital lived at Rogate-on-Sands and, in an emergency, was on call.

The surgeon, having removed his theatre garb, now strolled into the tiny side-ward and viewed the bandaged Blythe quizzically.

'A nice, sharp blade,' he observed. 'With luck, it won't leave much of a scar. The nose, perhaps. Maybe on the arm. But otherwise he'll soon be as good as new.'

The nurse fiddled with the drip that fed plasma into Blythe's unbandaged arm. Frieda Blythe did not take her eyes from the bandaged face of her husband. Nor did she ease the grasp on the Ventolin inhaler in her right hand.

'He'll be woozy for a while,' said the surgeon.

'I'd like to stay.'

'Of course.' The surgeon smiled. 'But there might be things you'd like to do. Notify somebody. Have a meal, perhaps. A couple of hours from now he'll know exactly what he's talking about.'

'We have no family, and very few friends.'

'Somebody, surely?'

'Nobody. We have no children. We've always found it difficult to make friends. We're not gregarious in any way.'

'Now that's a nice word for a sunny Sunday morning.'

The door of the side-ward was ajar and the woman stood there, watching the nurse, the surgeon and the wife of the injured man. Her eyes were red-rimmed.

161

Her face was a little pale and drawn. Before anybody could enquire as to her business, she introduced herself.

'Sylvia Walker. The fat policewoman . . .'

'Sergeant Grant?'

'She said you might be here. The bastard who did this to your husband killed mine.'

'Oh!'

The surgeon flicked his eyes between the faces of the two women. The nurse, apparently satisfied with the rate of drip, fiddled with the sheets and pillows and eased what creases there were out of them.

Sylvia Walker said, 'There's a café, Olde Worlde, not very far from here. It's nice. Select. They serve mid-morning snacks, toasted teacake and Earl Grey. I think you should come with me.'

'No. I'd —'

'I think you should,' echoed the surgeon.

Sylvia Walker said, 'As a favour to me. Please.'

Police Constable Tidy figured that for the first time since he'd arrived at Audsley Avenue the initiative was being removed from the coloured youth, Wallace. The SBS Marine sergeant seemed to know exactly what he was doing.

By this time a heavy, black plastic bin-bag had been tacked over the hole that had been blasted in the door of the bungalow. There had been token opposition to the placing of the blindfold; the snout of the shotgun had been poked tentatively at the plastic. But Littlewood had made a grab at the barrels, and they'd been hurriedly withdrawn. Now some sort of future strategy was being discussed, in barely audible whispers, alongside the door.

'The old boy.' Littlewood glanced towards the garden shed. 'Who is he?'

'Name of Gowan. Ex-Chief Superintendent, Hong

162

Kong Police.'

'And the other one. The one who's buckled?'

'One of our men, Inspector Fuller.' Then, almost protectively, 'He's a good man. It's just that the pressure was a little too heavy.'

'If you say so,' said Littlewood flatly. Then, still in a barely audible whisper, 'You're the runner. Okay? We'll work things out, and you can duck around to the various points and get things organised.'

Tidy hesitated, then whispered, 'Okay, I'll do my best. But remember, I don't carry rank.'

'Nor do I.' Littlewood allowed himself a mirthless grin. 'But those who do don't seem to be much sodding good.'

Tidy didn't answer.

'There's a front door,' continued Littlewood. 'He's not going to be allowed to use it. I want boxes, cardboard, old tyres, anything piled against it, then soaked with petrol. Tell whoever's there. If that door opens, they drop a match. When he comes out, if he comes out, it's through this door. And when *we* decide.'

They walked side by side along the pavement towards the café. They walked in step, and slowly. They talked in short sentences, and what they said had little real meaning except to themselves, but to them it was a screen – a shield – behind which they could each hide their personal distress.

Sylvia Walker said, 'I'm told it's a coloured man. From Liverpool.'

Frieda Blythe countered with: 'It doesn't do the coloured fraternity much good.'

'I hope it doesn't build up to riot proportions.'

'You think it might?'

'Think of Liverpool. It's very volatile.'

'It happened here, not in Liverpool.'

Sylvia Walker said, 'The average Scouse mentality.'

'You think so?'

'Hit first, think later.'

'Not all of them, surely.'

'Enough of a minority to create trouble.'

They reached a zebra crossing and Sylvia Walker pressed the button to show red to oncoming traffic. There was very little difference in their ages, but Walker had a natural, maternal air. She cupped her hand under the other woman's elbow, and Blythe did nothing to discourage her. They didn't speak again until they'd crossed the road.

Then Frieda Blythe asked, 'Do you have any family?'

'A daughter.'

'Oh! She should be—'

'She's in the Mediterranean, somewhere, bumming around on a leaking yacht, with a broken-down engine. With some cheap jerk who, like her, doesn't like work.'

'You don't—' Frieda Blythe hesitated, and said, 'You don't sound too keen.'

'Not since I found her in bed with my husband. And enjoying it.'

'Y'mean . . .'

'It's illegal, my pet. Father and daughter.'

'Oh!'

'But that doesn't mean it's so damned unusual.'

Frieda Blythe said 'Oh!' again.

They walked perhaps twenty yards in silence, then Sylvia Walker said, 'Strange. I hated her much more than I hated him.'

'I wouldn't – y'know—'

'I'm embarrassing you. I'm sorry.'

'It's all right. It's just that—'

'Men are bastards, anyway.'

'Not all of them.'

'Not yours, my pet.' And she sounded as if she meant

164

it. She again touched Frieda Blythe's elbow with her hand and said, 'Right. Here we are. My treat. It was my invitation.'

Tidy breathed, 'It's organised. Crates and boxes from The Jester's Bells. We're getting a couple of gallons of petrol from the garage in Audsley Crescent. And there's a squad car sergeant seeing it's all done efficiently.'

'Makes a change.' Littlewood was the complete professional. The impression was that this is what he was there for, what he'd trained for. Like a chess master, he seemed to be a few moves ahead of the play. He whispered, 'What's Fuller like? Is he still a passenger? Or has he pulled himself together?'

Tidy tended to argue. To excuse. He said, 'He's all right. He's a good officer. It's just that—'

'Okay. Just that I want somebody I can trust on that telephone when we move into action. And I want to know the exact location of the telephone inside the bungalow. Know that. Get him to answer and we know exactly where he is, even if we can't see him.'

Tidy nodded his understanding.

Littlewood continued, 'Pity we can't get a couple of stun grenades. That would really make him cough.' Then, after a pause, 'Laddo. Over there.' He gave a tiny gesture across the closed door.

'Y'mean Wragg? Segeant Wragg?'

'Is that his name? Get round to him. No heroics. He does what I tell him to do, when I tell him to do it. We've already had too much farting around. The bolts on the door haven't been shot. If he's used his ears, he'll know that. Just the latch-lock and the door knob. They're on his side of the door. We need a sledge-hammer or something like that. And when the time arrives we need this Wragg character to use it. Do what you can. Explain

165

it to him. And to whoever fancies using the telephone.'

'Right.'

'And emphasise, there's just the one chance. That's all we've got. Speed, surprise and timing. All three. Get one of them wrong and we have trouble.'

The body of Reginald Palfrey was washed up at the mouth of the River Ribble on the Tuesday. The tides and currents along that stretch of the coast can play strange tricks. On the Friday a coroner's inquest brought in a verdict of Accidental Death. Constable Daniels and Timothy Barstow were both called to give evidence and, although both of them told the truth, neither of them told the whole truth.

As a rider to the verdict the coroner criticised the Rogate-on-Sands Pier Company for not having a high enough guard rail around the sides and end of the pier.

Which was a little unfair.

The truth was that Palfrey had done everything with a quiet but determined deliberation. He had waited until the pier was as deserted as it was likely to become, in view of the time of the day. He had strolled, unhurriedly, to a secluded corner behind the unused pavilion. When he was sure nobody was watching he'd climbed to the top of the guard rail, balanced there for a moment, closed his eyes, then stepped forward into space.

Despite his calling, he hadn't even said a prayer. It had not seemed appropriate.

He might not have been dead when he hit the water, but he was certainly unconscious. The side of his head had smashed into the barnacle-encrusted upright of the pier.

Thereafter, nothing until his body was washed up at the mouth of the River Ribble two days later.

He wasn't even missed.

166

*

Fuller felt the shame hit him. As the trembling subsided the shame and self-disgust built up.

Gowan said, 'It's nothing. You've nothing to be ashamed of.'

'I cracked,' muttered Fuller.

'With justification.' Then Gowan smiled and said, 'You saved my life. I'm grateful for that, at any rate.'

'I'm supposed to be in charge here.' The revulsion he felt for himself rode Fuller's harsh tone. 'Other men – police officers – out there expect things to be under control. They're not and it's my fault.'

'What else?' Gowan made believe he was losing his patience with the younger man. 'You're not under the delusion you've got a bullet-proof navel, are you? He has a gun, and he's obviously prepared to use it. Our options are very limited.'

'My only option is to get that bastard into a police cell without anybody else being injured.'

'Easier said than done.'

'Nobody said it was easy.' Fuller was almost himself again. 'Just that it's going to be done.'

Tidy approached the shed from an angle and keeping his eye on the rear door of the bungalow. He ducked into the shadow of the shed and said, 'He seems to have worked something out.'

' "He"? who the hell's "he"?'

'The man in the blue jogging outfit.' Tidy's voice was tight and a little strained. 'He seems to know what he's doing.'

'A bloody Royal Marine sergeant. Since when did—'

'*It's about time somebody did!*' exploded Tidy. Then, in a slightly calmer but still angry tone, 'Inspector, I don't give a toss if he's in the Girl Guides. He seems capable of doing something more constructive than simply

167

standing there letting coppers be slashed to ribbons. And until such time as somebody comes up with some better ideas, I'll go along with his plan of action.'

Gowan looked unhappy, and said, 'Constable, I think you should—'

'And the same applies to you, mister.' Tidy turned onto the older man. 'This is a shambles, and if you'd the sense you were born with you'd recognise it as such. We have somebody who seems to know how to handle it. For Christ's sake, let him. It'll make a pleasant change.'

There were some moments of highly charged silence. Tidy realised that he'd gone beyond any reasonable limit. Fuller, too, realised that after his temporary crack-up he was in no position to make too many demands. And Gowan knew himself to be an elderly man, perhaps living a little too much in the past, and certainly without even token authority in the present circumstances. They were all in the wrong, but none of them was totally in the wrong. There was a silence which very gradually eased into an awkward discomfiture.

'What does he suggest?' ground Fuller.

'He wants you to use the telephone. He'll tell you when. To distract attention, I think. That, I gather, is when he's going in. To get the mad bastard under control.'


## 1100 Hours

Out to the west on the sea's horizon an occasional, handkerchief cloud peeped up, as if to check that it was safe to drift shorewards. Somewhere over the Atlantic a weather front was flexing its muscles. It was going to rain. Tomorrow, or the next day, the heavens would open up. Those on holiday were due a soaking and a grumbling. But that was tomorrow or maybe the next day, and today it was glorious holiday weather, and skins were browning and peeling, and pores were oozing sweat. And everybody made believe they were having the whale of a time.

Some men are born policemen. Before they can talk — before they can walk – they can handle a rattle with the assurance of a New York cop handling a night stick. They enter the world with the swaggering arrogance of a Met inspector approaching a skinhead. They are hard men and law-enforcement would be impossible without them.

Vic Wood was not such a man. He wore the uniform and he drew the pay, but there was no more.

He strolled his way from C Beat to A Beat for no better reason than a yen to walk along the prom. He chose back streets and short cuts: narrow alleys with cobbled surfaces, where dustbins were kept and few, if any, visitors ventured. Here, few incidents requiring the services of a constable might be encountered. Wood had skiving off to a fine art.

Crosby was safe; thanks to a sweetly timed bending of his automobile, Superintendent Crosby was well clear of the streets. Blythe, it would seem, was well taken care of; if all the flap and panic coming over the air waves via his personal radio was to be believed, Fuller and half the force were tooling around on D Beat. Indeed, if all the static pushed out by his walkie-talkie was to be believed, the last person they needed to arse things up generally in Audsley Avenue was PC Wood.

Therefore it was with a clear conscience that Wood came out of the back streets, crossed the carriageway, nipped through Rock Walk then sauntered peacefully south along the promenade, with the railings and the sea on his right.

It was nice, it was colourful (thanks to the gaily hued dresses of the ladies and the flash shirts of the men) and, above all else, it was peaceful. No hassle. Not too much noise. No likelihood of a hooligan needing to be brought under control. Just the scream of the gulls and the wash and splash of the waves against the face of the prom.

The face of the prom was not square to the incoming waves, and the water was getting deeper by the minute. The curl of the waves raced from north to south along the face of the prom. It was quite amazing how fast they raced, and quite suddenly Wood thought about Benjamin. He, too, had laughed and gurgled at the run of the waves.

Benjamin . . .

He would be seven years old now. No, eight. Going to school. No longer strapped in a baby carriage. He'd be past making sand-castles. He wouldn't be quite the innocent he'd once been.

Wood hoped that Benjamin's step-father was as kind a man as he'd seemed. Not Judy. He didn't give a damn about Judy. Judy had shown what she was. What Aunt Amy would have called a flibbertigibbet. Too flighty ever to be taken seriously.

And yet he'd taken her seriously. Too seriously. He'd married her, honestly believing they could make a go of it. And he'd tried. Harder than he'd ever tried in his life.

He'd been a fair-to-middling copper in those days, too. Not a great policeman. He could never be that. Maybe not even a good policeman. But he'd tried to pull his weight. He'd tried not to be a passenger. In those days he'd have been in Audsley Avenue. He'd have been at least trying.

Wood had stopped to stare out to sea with unseeing eyes. He was jerked out of his revery by the stranger's question.

'Is it the Isle of Man, then?'

170

'Eh?' Wood turned his head and saw a little old man wearing a coloured, make-believe baseball cap.

'You're looking out there.' The little old man nodded towards the sea's skyline. 'Is that the Isle of Man you can see?'

'The Welsh hills,' said Wood.

'Oh!'

'There.' Wood raised an arm and pointed to his right. 'The Lake District hills, sometimes. They're sometimes very plain.'

'But not the Isle of Man?' The little old man sounded disappointed.

'Sorry. It's just too far away.'

The Jester's Bells had opened its doors for business. It was the sort of hostelry that seemed to have a surfeit of Formica tops, green leather and chrome. It also had a juke-box contraption that was already getting into serious competition with the build-up of conversation. Nevertheless the babble of talk rose and fell and, as was to be expected, focused on one subject.

'From what I can see they're going to burn him out.'

'Y'mean set fire to the bungalow?'

'That's what it looks like.'

' . . . and Arkwright always was a bit of a strange bird.'

'I know. Very sly.'

'It's not that I'm surprised. Just that you don't expect things like that here, at Rogate.'

'It can happen anywhere.'

'But *dope*. I mean you can't visualise—'

'I mean, he can't complain. If he's up to the eyes in dope running, what can he—'

'I only hope they keep the fire under control.'

The main bar was filling up with media people, too. They added to the hubbub as they expressed opinions and sought new angles to the Audsley Avenue situation.

'Did I hear somebody mention dope?'

'That's what they say. That, and an arms cache for the IRA.'

'Not just hot air? It's not just speculation?'

'A pretty firm piece of information.'

'Heroin or cocaine?'

'I can't see old man Arkwright having anything to do with the people who—'

'It's quite amazing how many policemen they can come up with at a time like this.'

'The IRA?'

'They've got to be *somewhere*.'

'I hope to God they have the Fire Brigade standing by if they're going to burn them out.'

'I knew there was something funny about Arkwright.'

'You never think it's going to happen in your neighbourhood.'

The speculation and the rumours jostled each other in the confines of the bar and the lounge. The conjecture and the guesses, the suppositions and the theories, the assumptions and the fancies. Facts and knowledge sank within an ocean of wild imagination. As long as they lived these people would know the happenings of that morning as The Siege of Audsley Avenue.

Tidy and the SBS sergeant, Littlewood, had moved a couple of feet to one side of the rear door of the bungalow. They were (hopefully) within jumping distance, but out of earshot. They spoke in whispers.

Tidy said, 'These,' and held out a box containing half-a-dozen of what looked to be stubby fireworks. 'Anti-mole smoke bombs. I found them under the bench in the greenhouse. If we can get a couple into the rear hall—'

'We'll get them in,' said Littlewood. Then, 'What about the telephone? Do we know the exact location?'

172

'One of the neighbours,' whispered Tidy. 'It's an L-shaped hall. The phone's on the wall on the inside of the elbow. About twelve foot from the door.' He added, 'I couldn't find a sledge-hammer. There was a woodman's axe.' His lips bowed into a quick grin. 'Sergeant Wragg's eager to use it.'

'When I say when.'

'Of course.'

'And the other one? By the field telephone?'

'They'll go along.' Then Tidy added, 'I brought this along. If we ever get near enough to use it, it'll stop a few arguments.'

'This' was an ancient butcher's cleaver. Its blade was chipped and serrated from mis-use – chopping firewood and the like – but as a close-quarter weapon it was a fearsome thing.

Littlewood held out his hand and said, 'I'll take it.'

'Look, I'm not too anxious—'

'I'll take it,' repeated Littlewood. 'You'll be busy lighting these smoke bombs. And anyway you might hesitate before using it. Not me, boy. I'll chop his bloody head off as soon as look at him.'

Still with some reluctance, Tidy handed him the cleaver.

Littlewood weighed it in his right hand, then said, 'Right. Now we give him a slice of meditative silence. Then, when he thinks we've dropped off, we go. We all go!'

'You realise I'm scared stupid, of course.'

Sylvia Walker spoke the words softly, immediately before biting into a piece of toasted and well-buttered teacake. She'd remained silent for the last five minutes or so, as if screwing up her courage to make the quietly spoken admission.

Frieda Blythe murmured, 'Aren't we all?'

173

'No, I mean it. I'm talking about being scared rotten.'

It was an old-fashioned café. It had tiny tables, whose surfaces were covered with spotlessly white table-cloths. It had silver cutlery, white but obviously expensive crockery and bowls of cube sugar on each table. It had small, elegantly framed hunting scenes on the wall and what looked to be genuine rafters across the ceiling. It specialised in buttered teacake and creamy, rich gateaux.

Frieda Blythe sipped at her tea and waited for the other woman to continue.

Sylvia Walker chewed, swallowed, then took a mouthful of her tea before she spoke.

She said, 'I make enemies a lot easier than I make friends.'

'You didn't do too badly just now.' Frieda Blythe smiled. 'I didn't even know you before you arrived at the hospital.'

'That's different.'

'Surely not.'

'If your husband—' Sylvia Walker hesitated, then started again. 'Your husband's slashed and mine's been killed. If that hadn't happened, I wouldn't have thanked you for friendship.'

'Oh!'

'It's my way. I'm sorry. I'm glad now, of course I am, but if things hadn't happened . . .'

Frieda Blythe paused, then said, 'You live alone, right?'

'Of course.'

'Who are you going to let know? About your husband, I mean?'

'Nobody. I have nobody.'

'You have a daughter.'

'She doesn't count.'

'Look, you can't—'

'She doesn't count.' She repeated the words through clenched teeth. Then, 'What *she* did. What *he* did.'

'You can't hate forever.'

'I can have a damned good try.'

Frieda Blythe reached down and lifted her handbag from where she had placed it, by her ankle, when they'd arrived.

She asked, 'Do you smoke?'

'It's a filthy habit.'

'Of course.'

'Disgusting and unhealthy.'

'Quite. But do you?'

'I stopped some months ago.'

'I'm going to have a cigarette,' said Frieda Blythe. 'I rarely do, but this time . . .' She opened her handbag and produced a packet of cigarettes. 'I won't press, but I think you should, too.'

Sylvia Walker helped herself to one of the cigarettes offered and held it in the flame of the lighter thumbed into life by the other woman.

Frieda Blythe put away the cigarettes and the lighter, and they both inhaled and exhaled before Sylvia Walker spoke.

She said, 'Bad habit or not, I needed that.'

'We'll have a re-fill,' said Frieda Blythe. 'Then we'll both go back to the hospital.'

'There's no need for me to go. I'll just—'

'We'll both go back to the hospital,' insisted Frieda Blythe. 'We'll check that Joe's okay and comfortable. Then we'll go to your place and collect some things.'

'Things?'

'Nighties, whatever you sleep in. We have a spare bedroom.'

'Look, I'm not asking for—'

'But I am. Maybe I'm not as tough as you. I don't like the idea of being alone for the next few days.'

175

Sylvia Walker drew on the cigarette, and her softly spoken, 'You may regret this,' came out wrapped in cigarette smoke.

'I may. But it's a risk I'm prepared to take.'

'I'll say it – then I can say "I told you so" – you're a soft-hearted fool.'

'Good.' Frieda Blythe smiled. 'The world needs its quota of fools. If only to encourage others to feel intelligent.'


## 1115 Hours

Daisy figured she'd had quite an adventure. Instead of the boring old paddock and the limited company of her fellow-mokes, she'd had a quiet walk in the small hours through deserted streets. She'd scoffed flowers and leaves with a taste that had been new to her, and even though the result had been a temporary belly-ache it had all added spice to what was becoming a very boring way of life.

Tomorrow, she'd be back on the sands. Waiting, head down and with infinite patience, for some dim-witted kid to be lifted astride her back in order to play Cowboys and Indians while she trotted the required run and back.

She didn't really mind when the little horrors kicked their heels into her ribs in the approved giddy-up manner. More often than not they were wearing either sandals or trainers, and if they even looked as if they might hurt the little chap at the other end of the rope halter – the guy who was leading her back to the paddock – would soon put a stop to things.

It was not too bad a life.

And now, if the truth were told, she was glad to be returning to her paddock. To doze away the rest of this

176

Sunday and get ready for the Monday morning spell, while the tide was out. It had been nice but the quiet life might, after all, be the best.

Detective Sergeant James Wragg had never felt like he felt at that moment. Never, in the whole of his life, would he feel that way again. He was alive as never before; the flow of adrenalin was giving him the confidence of scalpel sharpness. As he weighed the woodman's axe and prepared to explode into action, his gaze never left the man in the blue track-suit. Tidy, too, watched, as did Fuller and Gowan. It was moving towards midday – the morning would soon be part of history – and in some mysterious way Marine Sergeant Littlewood had taken a firm grip of events and seemed quite capable of resolving things his way.

Tidy was waiting. He held four of the smoke bombs in his hand, ready to pass them to Littlewood.

Littlewood tucked the ancient cleaver under his arm, took out a box of matches, then signalled to Fuller.

Fuller lifted the receiver of the field telephone and at the same time Littlewood struck a match into flame and touched the tops of the smoke bombs. From inside the bungalow the telephone started to ring. One at a time the smouldering fuses of the smoke bombs spurted into tiny flame, prior to emitting thick, yellow smoke.

The ringing of the telephone stopped. From behind the closed door Wragg and Littlewood could hear the mumble of Wallace's answering voice. Logic insisted that he was as far from the door as the entrance hall would allow and that at least one of his hands was occupied.

Littlewood reached across, took the smoking mole bombs from Tidy and jerked a corner of the black, plastic bin-bag clear of the hole the shotgun blast had blown in the door. One at a time, he tossed the smoke

177

bombs into the rear hall of the bungalow, then allowed the plastic to fall back into place and stepped out of firing line of the door. He held out a hand to quieten Wragg and a high-pitched, hiccuping howl came from an activated smoke detector.

Littlewood grinned and murmured, 'A bonus.'

Wallace's voice fell silent. A second later, the corner of the black plastic moved as one of the smoke bombs was thrown out of the bungalow. The plastic moved a second time, but this time Littlewood slashed downward with the cleaver.

Had the cleaver been as sharp as it should have been fingers would have been chopped off. As it was skin and flesh were sliced and ripped to the bone. A scream of pain came from inside the bungalow. Littlewood yelled, '*Now!*' and Wragg swung the woodman's axe.

It was a good, full-blooded, well-aimed blow and the woodwork around the lock shattered. The door flew inwards and Littlewood, followed by Tidy and Wragg, burst into the passage-like hall.

The two police officers grabbed at Wallace's arms and wrenched the shotgun from his grasp. Littlewood dodged to a position behind the coloured man, clamped a neck-lock on from the rear and . . .

Later, when telling of the incident to a small but select band of friends, Wragg described it this way. It was a little like walking through a wood in autumn, the leaves thick and rotting underfoot. Then, suddenly, unexpectedly, a hidden branch beneath a thickness of those leaves snaps with the pressure of a footstep.

That was the sound. A crack; plain enough to hear, but well muffled.

The coloured man suddenly stopped resisting the pull and tug of Wragg and Tidy. He went limp then fell forward, out of the door, down the steps and onto the path. He fell into some of the congealed blood and the blood from his injured hand added to the blood already there. He ended up at the feet of the newly arrived Fuller.

Wragg and Tidy staggered down the steps of the bungalow, coughing. Littlewood disappeared into the bungalow. Fuller bent down and felt for the pulse at Wallace's jaw.

Fuller straightened, then said, 'He's dead.'

'Is he?' Wragg showed the minimum of interest.

'How?'

'He fell awkwardly.'

'Dammit, he couldn't—'

'He fell,' interrupted Tidy. 'Awkwardly. *Very* awkwardly.'

'I don't—'

'What you *didn't* see was what he did to Johnny Walker. If you want, I'll subscribe to a wreath. Other than that, don't ask me to be concerned.' Tidy's tone was hard and without compassion. He ended, 'He's dead. He lived long enough to cause a lot of trouble. He should have died sooner.'

'If there's an enquiry—'

'If there's an enquiry,' cut in Wragg, 'if questions are asked, they'll all be answered. He fell *awkwardly*. Now, for Christ's sake, leave it.'

Fuller blew out his cheeks and looked worried, but remained silent.

Tidy said, 'Somebody who knows about these things. Get them to switch that smoke detector contraption off.'

'I'll do that,' volunteered Wragg. He moved towards the rear door of the bungalow.

Gowan joined Fuller and Tidy.

As Wragg entered Littlewood came out of the bungalow, holding the arm of a middle-aged woman who was holding a handkerchief to her nose as a counter to the smoke. Littlewood was fairly beaming his pleasure.

179

He said, 'She was hiding in a wardrobe.'

'I was hiding in the wardrobe,' she echoed. 'I heard the man breaking in and I couldn't get out. I couldn't get to the telephone. I was scared. So I hid in the wardrobe.'

She seemed proud, even delighted with her presence of mind.

In a weary voice Fuller said, 'We'll need a statement. From both of you.'

'Not from me,' said Littlewood.

'Look, don't start all that—'

'I'm not allowed to. It's that simple. When I get back to the depot I'll report to my Commanding Officer. He'll contact your Chief Constable.'

Fuller looked dissatisfied but didn't push things.

The scream of the smoke detector stopped and Wragg joined them.

Gowan said, 'The press. I think you should fob them off with something, Inspector. If not, some of them will invent their own stories.'

'Right.' Fuller squared his shoulders a little. He gave instructions to Tidy. 'You. Take the Sergeant and his aunty back to his aunt's house. Then nip home, get cleaned up, then report back at the police station and start the paperwork.' To Littlewood and the woman he said, 'Go with him, in his van. Say nothing to the reporters. Nothing! And duck the cameras as much as possible. We'll be in touch with your Commanding Officer. Not me, but somebody with some weight on his shoulders. And you,' to the woman. 'We will have a statement from you. A policewoman will call later today.'

Tidy, Littlewood and the woman moved off towards Tidy's van. Fuller turned to Gowan.

He said, 'Old man, we owe you thanks. I owe you thanks. Hang around. I'll give you a lift to the police station, then we'll need a statement from you.'

Then, to Wragg, 'It's all yours, Sergeant. Here in particular. Get the whole three-ring-circus out. Photography Section. Fingerprint Section. Sketch Plan Section. Serious Crime. Forensic. The lot. Make a meal of it. Give the ratepayers value for money. Shift the body. Notify the coroner. When you've got things under way, give me a ring. I'll be in my office, sorting out that end of things. I'll get onto the Liverpool boys and start working out his next-of-kin.' Then, in disgust, as a Rover nosed its way past the police line, 'And *that* is all we need. A dopy prat of an Assistant Chief Constable, arriving when everything's sewn up.'

\* \* \*

And that was the end of it.

We-ell, not quite.

There were some loose ends. But there are always loose ends. To everything.

Take the identity of the coloured man whose neck Littlewood had snapped. It might have been Wallace. It might not. The Liverpool police could shed no light on the subject. Fingerprints were taken, a corpse-shot was circulated, but without success. Three days after the incident the coroner – an elderly, retired medic who lived in a perpetual state of high dudgeon – was most irate when he had to open and adjourn the inquest because nobody could identify the body. The dead man was stored in a freezing drawer in the hospital morgue. Then, three months later, still without a clue to his identity, the dead man was buried in a corner of the municipal cemetery, a corner originally reserved for paupers and suicides.

Or take Crosby.

He was charged and tried for a moderately serious

181

road traffic offence, Driving Without Due Care And Attention, and he was fined fifty pounds. He was very miffed; miffed enough to proffer his resignation, even more miffed when it was accepted without a word.

But on the strength of his past rank and authority he was offered a sit-down job by a small-time, local security firm. His name appeared on the firm's notepaper as the 'Crime Prevention Consultant'.

He is thinking about standing for councillor at the next local election. That's how much spare time he has.

And, finally . . .

About twenty-four hours after the incident the Chief Constable was required to go to London. To the Home Office. He was met by a senior official, and an equally senior official from the Ministry of Defence.

The meeting lasted less than thirty minutes, and what was said has always remained highly confidential.

Nevertheless the Chief Constable returned home, sent for the Assistant Chief Constable and officially slammed the door on any further enquiries into the matter. The Assistant Chief Constable was very annoyed, but who gives a damn about Assistant Chief Constables?

Little, Brown now offers an exciting range of quality titles by
both established and new authors. All of the books in this
series are available by faxing, or posting your order to:

Little, Brown and Company (UK) Limited
Mail order,
P.O. Box 11,
Falmouth,
Cornwall, TR10 9EN
Fax: 0326-376423

Payments can be made as follows: Cheque, postal order
(payable to Little, Brown Cash Sales) or by credit cards,
Visa/Access/Mastercard. Do not send cash or currency.
U.K.customers and B.F.P.O.; Allow £1.00 for postage and
packing for the first book, plus 50p for the second book,
plus 30p for each additional book up to a maximum charge
of £3.00 (7 books plus) U.K. orders over £75 free postage
and packing.

Overseas customers including Ireland, please allow £2.00 for
postage and packing for the first book, plus £1.00 for the
second book, plus 50p for each additional book.

NAME (Block Letters)

........................................................................................

ADDRESS

........................................................................................

........................................................................................

........................................................................................

☐ I enclose my remittance for ............................................

☐ I wish to pay by Visa/Access/Mastercard

Number ☐☐☐☐☐☐☐☐☐☐☐☐☐☐☐

Card Expiry Date ☐☐☐☐